CW00858636

Can You Teach an Old Dog New Tricks?

Lottie Heritage

To Colin, Jack and Lizzy.

I'm so lucky and proud that you are my family.

Chapter 1

Red Nose Syndrome

Gemma was concentrating hard, so hard that her tongue was out and her brow furrowed. She was on her third nose-warmer design and was quite determined that this one would work. Being nine, Gemma knew that anything was possible. There was no problem that couldn't be solved in the whole world - all that was needed was determination and a little ingenuity. Her first nose-warmer design had been made out of a piece of cloth, fitted to the peak of a black cap. The cloth was then attached around the back of her head, using a piece of elastic that had previously been used to hold up her hockey socks. Even though the design helped to cure her cold nose syndrome, her mum said that the post-box-shaped eye hole made her look like a ninja, and that this was *'inappropriate'* for walking to school. Gemma didn't agree that looking like a ninja was a problem at all; in fact, she felt oddly cool wearing it. However, it was not being able to see properly while wearing Nose Warmer 0.1 that put her off, especially on days when there were snowball fights.

Gemma usually walked to school alone. While walking, she would drift off into her own world and conjure up inventions in her head. Because she was always busy in her head, thinking up new schemes for this, and new inventions for that, she often forgot that there may be people watching her. As she walked, she regularly chatted loudly to herself, or shouted 'Aaah HA' as a super new invention filled her mind.

The local bullies, known as 'T's Gang', often shouted rude comments back at Gemma, but they hadn't approached her recently since she'd embarrassed them one day. T's Gang had waited for Gemma. Four of the gang were skulking under the canal bridge so as not to be detected by passers by. Another two boys were waiting on the top of the bridge. They were the heavy mob who would capture Gemma and deliver her to the skulkers under the bridge. As Gemma crossed the top of the bridge, the two boys pulled her by her rucksack and her arm, and shoved her down the three, small steps until she was under the bridge, where she was then surrounded by the rest of the gang.

But as Gemma was in 'Gemma's world', she didn't take much notice of what was happening. She was so deep in thought that she wasn't afraid at all. Usually, T's Gang got exactly what they wanted because their victims were scared, but Gemma didn't cotton on to the fact that she was a victim at all. Without a thought, she simply pointed her finger out towards a beautiful heron that was landing on the tow path, just behind the group of bullies. All of the gang turned to look at what she was pointing at, and Gemma casually turned around and walked away. This was a huge embarrassment for the gang. They hadn't even pushed or shoved her around before clever Gemma had managed to escape, without a single demand for lunch money or sweets being issued!

Anyway, back to this nose warmer thingy. You've probably guessed by now that ever since she could remember, Gemma had detested the way her nose looked when it was cold. She hated how it turned red and shiny on cold days - not a good look for anyone. Her second nose-warmer design, called 0.2, was, well, what could only really be described as a nose scarf. Gemma invented it after she'd used her school scarf to cover her neck, mouth and nose one day, and found that this did the trick. By the time she got to school, her nose was not its usual red-almost-turning-blue colour, it was just a glorious normal pink like everyone else's. There was also a distinct lack of bulbous shine. Ever since someone had commented that she looked like Rudolph in training, she was now trying to avoid the red, bulbous, shine at all costs. However, even though she was pleased by the results from wearing the scarf, this solution was far from perfect, as she absolutely couldn't bear the feeling of her wet breath on her scarf and on her chin. It reminded her of how, when there was even the smallest speck of something messy on her face, her mum would lunge at her with a pre-licked tissue, grabbing her chin in a 'don't you even think about trying to turn your head around' kind of way. Then, she would rub furiously at the offending mess, like it was a piece of dog poo or other such substance that could not possibly be witnessed by any other member of the human race.

Gemma often wondered about things like why adults get so upset about little bits of tomato, or pasta, or ice cream, or chocolate, or chewing gum, or toffee apple, or anything else, yes, even dog poo resting on your face. Why do they have to scrub you like your cheek is the bottom of a really, really dirty pan, until the offending food's been removed, to be replaced by an equally offending red mark? Why do they think it's better for you to live with that disgusting smell of their spit under your nose all day, instead of a little bit of yummy food? How do adults manage to eat their dinner without getting any on their shirt or face? Is it some kind of magic trick that you only learn when you're grown up?

So, going back to version 0.2, Gemma decided that a nose scarf was a possible solution to red nose syndrome. She took an old sock, it was a long, vomit-coloured hockey sock that had lost its brother or sister, presumably devoured by the great sock-eating monster living in the washing machine and she cut it exactly in half. At this stage of the design, Nose Warmer 0.2 now looked like a pair of long puppy-dog ears. Gemma then took one of the puppy-dog ears and cut it in half again. I know you're thinking about cutting up puppy-dog ears now, but I've already told you it's really just a single, old, miserable sock, so keep your mind on the story. Now, version 0.2 was really beginning to take shape. Gemma took her strip of sock and placed it around the back of her head. Then, she brought the two ends over each ear, towards her face, tying them together in a knot on her nose.

As Gemma looked into the mirror, she howled with laughter at herself. I know that the howling has reminded you of the puppy-dog again, but please let it go now! Anyway, forgetting the ridiculous fashion faux pas that was sitting on her face, Gemma decided to concern herself with the practicalities of the design, and to test to see if it met her specification.

1. Was her nose warm? Yes, although this was not really a fair test as she was actually indoors with the heating on.
2. Could she see incoming snowballs while wearing version 0.2? Yes.

3. Was it easy to use? Yes.

4. Did it look completely ridiculous and draw unwanted attention? Yes.

5. Would she be using this on her journey to school in the morning? Yes, but not until she'd figured out a way of fixing Point 4.

So, standing at the mirror with a very warm nose, Gemma carefully slid the knot from her nose, around to the back of her head, making it a little less obvious and perhaps a little less odd to look at. This worked very well, even if the action of moving the knot made her nose flat and her face sore. So now, Gemma was pleased with 0.2 and decided that the best storage place was around her neck, after all, it was technically a scarf. She slid the nose scarf down, off her nose and over her mouth until it rested quite comfortably around her neck. This was a perfect solution to bulbous red nose syndrome. Gemma was very pleased with 0.2 and was definitely going to test it out on the way to school tomorrow.

The day of testing had arrived, Gemma carefully lifted 0.2 from her bedside table, and did her best to tie a knot behind her head. As she was tying, she noticed little bits of vomit-coloured thread dangling in all directions from the nose scarf. She also quickly realised that once socks have begun to fray, they really don't know when to stop! Being as careful as she could with 0.2 in place, she set out for school hoping that she would arrive with a lovely, normal pink nose just like all the other children. However,

0.2 didn't want to play. And soon, Gemma had long trails of sickly-coloured thread dangling down her face. Every time she breathed in, bits of thread would weave their way into her mouth, and she had to spit them out. At some point, two pieces of thread joined forces; one wrapped itself around her tongue, while the other shot up her left nostril, making her cough and sneeze all at the same time! Now, the irritating, tickly, distracting, uncomfortable, dangly threads were covered in snot and spit and proved to be a worse combination than the original wet-breath-scarf. Gemma, being Gemma, continued to wear 0.2 all the way to school as having a pretty pink nose was still all important, and no one could ever call Gemma a quitter!

When she arrived at school, she began the messy task of taking 0.2 off her nose. Which way should she go? Should she stick with her original plan and wear it around her neck, or pull it over her head? Either way she would end up covered in snot. Gemma decided to lift 0.2 upwards and over her head - at least this way she wouldn't have to sit with snot around her neck all day. Now that that decision was made, it was most important to perform this delicate operation in front of a mirror. What colour would her nose be? She made her way through the school gates and directly to the mirror in the toilet block. This was the moment of truth! Would it be red and bulbous or pretty and pink? Gemma carefully lifted her nose scarf to find a lovely, pink, matt nose sitting inside. There was a slight ridge across the centre where 0.2

had sat, but that didn't matter to Gemma at all as she was very pleased with her pink nose, and immediately began to invent 0.3 in her head. She knew that the next version would need to be fray proof, but at this stage was a little unsure of how to achieve it.

Chapter 2

Sal's Sandwiches

The school day was pretty average. Gemma hung out with Sal and Greg during break time, and at lunch time they played the Guess The Ingredients in Sal's Sandwich game. Sal's mum had a habit of making the most bizarre sandwiches, often consisting of left overs from dinner, so the sandwiches sometimes contained chopped-up sprouts or risotto! 'Waste not, want not' was Sal's mum's favourite saying. Today it turned out that Sal had parsnip and stuffing sandwiches. She loved them and offered to share, but both Gemma and Greg declined her generous offer.

There were a few times that Sal had been unable to eat her lunch; this was when the excitement about Guess the Ingredients in Sal's Sandwich was at its highest. Sometimes, no matter how hard they tried, they couldn't guess what mystery food Sal's mum had squashed between the bread. Occasionally, the strange combinations were a little unpalatable and even Sal couldn't face eating them! When this happened, Gemma and Greg always shared their lunch with Sal, and were often surprised the

following day when Sal revealed what the food had actually been.

Their most memorable sandwich to date was one that Sal brought for lunch the day after her birthday. It consisted of spaghetti Bolognese sauce, Sal's favourite meal in the whole wide world, sprinkled with hundreds and thousands from her birthday cake, intermingled with grated cheese and crisps. Sal loved it. Her mum had even put a candle in with the sandwiches to remind her where the ingredients had come from. The reason that this was so memorable was that Sal's mum had wrapped similar sandwiches in serviettes for her to share with Gemma and Greg too. After all, it did contain some element of cake!

Gemma had made a list of Sal's incredible sandwiches to date:

- Rice pudding sandwich – this looked and smelled like gloopy wallpaper paste. No one believed that it was edible.
- Mashed potato and ketchup sandwich - it could only be described as a car crash oozing out a red mushy substance that vaguely resembled something you might find seeping from a zombie.
- Lychee and pasta sandwich – the lychees resembled slippery sheep eyes and the pasta was slimy, soggy and stringy. This reminded Sal of a TV programme she had seen where they pulled the guts out of a cow and she couldn't put the sandwich anywhere near her

mouth without getting that retching feeling. You know, that feeling you get when food wants to come out of your stomach and mouth, rather than the yummy chocolate feeling that makes you want to put food into your mouth and stomach.

On the way home from school, Gemma was busy inventing 0.3 in her head when something distracted her from her thoughts.

'Gem, GEM, GEMMMMAAAA!' she heard a familiar voice calling from behind. She turned to see Greg trotting untidily towards her, his bag in a tangle around his neck, and his coat draped upside down over his arm with the collar dragging on the floor. Greg always looked a state, his shirt untucked and his dark hair a mess no matter what time of day. Gemma loved his carefree approach to life. He never worried about silly stuff like parents do. Who cares if your hair's a mess? It still keeps your head warm. Who cares if your shoes are dirty? You walk on the floor in them and if you clean them, they're only going to get dirty again, it's the floor! These were the sorts of things that Greg would mumble to his teachers when they instructed him to 'Make yourself look presentable, young man!' However, there was one thing that Greg worried about, and that was being late. He hated it. He always wore a watch and always knew what time it was.

'Gem, have you seen the competition at the big arena? I'm going to enter it, well, me and Baldy, I'm gonna train him up so that we can win a trophy and get into the newspaper and everything,' said Greg.

'What competition are you on about?'

'It's in three weeks' time - you have to get your dog to follow you around a dog assault course and jump through hoops and balance and things, just like police dogs do. Annnnnd the best dog wins an awesome trophy.'

Gemma stopped walking and looked at Greg with an amazed expression on her face.

'Seriously, Baldy won't even sit when you tell him to, and he's so fat he'd probably get stuck inside the hoop!' chuckled Gemma.

'I know, but I've always wanted to train him to be a good dog. I'm sure he can do it, and if I show him the picture of the trophy it might help him to get better at dog things.'

'Do you really think that showing Baldy a picture of a trophy will inspire him to become a dog gymnast?'

'Yes I do, it's a very nice trophy,' said Greg in his most determined voice.

Gemma smiled and offered to help Greg in his dog training mission. She really wasn't keen on Baldy at all, but Greg was her best friend so she wanted to support him.

'I'm going to start training him tonight. I'll cut the picture of the competition winner's trophy out, and stick it up above his feeding bowl in the kitchen. That's a good place to start I think. Do you want to come and help me, Gem? I know you two haven't seen eye to eye since Baldy bit you, but he was only a puppy and he was scared. He did look really funny when the vet shaved all of the fur off his back, but when you let out that mega loud laugh he got spooked. The vet had to do something to get rid of the chewing gum he'd rolled in at the park - the poor pup was sticking to everything. He had bits of chewing gum and half a banana stuck to his back, cuz he'd been doing his daily bin sniff.'

Baldy was not really called Baldy at all. He was a two-year-old brown-and-white Jack Russell dog who was unsurprisingly named Jack to begin with. However, since his chewing gum incident at the park, Jack had been nick-named Baldy and this seemed to suit him better. Although to be honest, you could call him whatever you liked, Jack, Baldy, deaf dog, fatty, smelly bum - he didn't respond to anything!

'Erm, OK, I'll ask if I can come over later. I can bring my hula hoop for Baldy to jump through if you want?'

'Yeah, that's a great idea, see you later.'

*

Greg walked up the small path that led to his house and Baldy was lazily snoozing in the doorway.

'Baldy, BALDY, come here, Baldy,' called Greg enthusiastically, while patting his legs to attract the dog's attention.

Baldy showed no sign of getting up. The only movement he made was a quick tail wag, after he'd opened one eyelid, to see that it was Greg, and then closed the eyelid in order to go straight back to sleep. Greg was undeterred; he ruffled the top of Baldy's head as he arrived at his front door and told him he'd be back in five minutes.

*

Gemma arrived at Greg's house and, of course, Baldy was still in exactly the same spot, lazily snoozing the day away and getting fatter by the minute. The only time that Baldy really moved at all was from his basket to his feeding bowl, or from his feeding bowl to his front door spot, if the sun was shining there. He lived a millionaire lifestyle; he was fed and cared for, and everyone around him did everything for him.

'Living the dream, Baldy,' Gemma mumbled as she reached up to ring the door bell. Greg answered the door and patted Baldy on his sleepy head as he invited Gemma into the house.

'So, have you worn poor Baldy out with his training regime?' Gemma asked, knowing full well that the dog hadn't moved a muscle for four hours solid.

'Erm, I'm not sure that Baldy's ready for army style training yet, Gem, but I have put the picture of the trophy above his bowl so that he can see the prize!' answered Greg excitedly.

'Hmm, maybe I didn't need to bring my hoop today then,' mumbled Gemma.

Greg and Gemma spent the next two hours trying to convince Baldy that he *needed* to run around the garden and become a fit and obedient dog. They made a makeshift dog-sized see-saw out of house bricks and a plank of wood, but Baldy wouldn't go near the contraption. The only thing he moved for was food. Gemma suggested that if they put a doggy choc on the high end of the see-saw, Baldy might be tempted to go and get it. Greg thought this was a super idea, but Baldy simply walked to his full dog bowl and ate the doggy chocs out of there. It was far easier than climbing a rickety rackety plank, precariously balanced on some old house bricks. Still undeterred, Greg placed Gemma's hula hoop over Baldy and his feeding bowl to show the dog what it felt like to be inside a hoop. Baldy showed absolutely no interest in this at all; he finished his doggy chocs and sauntered off to his basket for yet another snooze.

Greg thought that for the first training session it had all gone rather well. Gemma, on the other hand, was not convinced at all. Putting a hoop over a dog was a million miles away from a dog voluntarily jumping through a hoop, but she didn't say this to

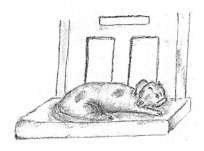

Greg. *There must be some way to motivate this dog,* thought Gemma, and she decided that she would think about this, once she had completed her design for 0.3.

Chapter 3

Success?

A few unremarkable days passed and Gemma asked Greg how things were coming along with Baldy. Greg was still very excited and asked her if she would come over one evening to check out their progress.

'Oh, is Baldy climbing the see-saw and jumping through the hoop now?' asked Gemma with a happy surprised kind of voice.

'Not exactly by himself yet, but I'm sure he will,' replied Greg with a huge smile across his dirty face.

While it appeared that Greg was making little progress with Project Baldy, Gemma was having considerable success with 0.3. She had decided that she needed to make a nose cap this time. The nose scarf had worked, in as much as she arrived at school with a lovely pink nose, but the design was slightly flawed by the snot, spit, fray and choke incident. So, on a piece of A4 paper, Gemma had drawn out her design, and was looking for the right materials to make it from. She had even gone as far as photocopying her design, and cutting it out of paper to make sure that it actually fitted her nose correctly. After first inspection, she decided that it fitted well enough. Now, what to make it out of?

Snow had started to fall and Gemma was in a rush to complete 0.3. To begin with she tried to make it out of wool. She began to knit some beautiful pink wool that she'd found in her mum's sewing drawer and soon realised that she couldn't knit a circle, she could only knit a square. However, Gemma loved the pink wool so much she pursued this by searching 'how to knit a circle' on her phone. She found an article on crocheting - a type of knitting done using a single hook instead of two needles. Gemma had no idea how to crochet, so the following day she put a sign up on the school notice board that read as follows:

HELP PLEASE
DO YOU KNOW HOW TO CROCHET?
I NEED TO MAKE A VERY SMALL NOSE-SHAPED SHAPE, CAN YOU HELP ME PLEASE?
Gemma – 5Z, Mr Prince's class
(Mr Prince can't crochet).

After placing her advertisement, Gemma thought that she would have to wait weeks before getting a reply. But, to her surprise, there was a note for her in the afternoon register asking her to go and see Mr Frazor, the caretaker, as he might be able to help her. Mr Prince, Gemma's teacher, read the message out and mumbled something about Gemma being in trouble for walking on the grass again, even though Gemma had never been in trouble for walking on the grass before!

Gemma couldn't help but wonder to herself why teachers with nice names were horrible, and teachers with horrible names were nice. She remembered being told that she was going into Mr Prince's class and was captivated by his name. She imagined that he would be tall, dark and, well, princely! Mr Prince was in fact, short, grey, had stained yellow teeth and was very boring. He had been a teacher all his working life and was no longer interested in anything the children had to say, or indeed anything that he should be teaching them. When children told him stories about things that they were excited about he just nodded and said 'mm' where he thought an 'mm' should go. Because he wasn't listening, he often got his 'mms' in the wrong place. One time when he was on playground duty, a child told him that he was feeling poorly and asked Mr Prince if he could go home. The usual reply of 'mm' followed, and the five-year-old boy climbed over the gate and started to walk home, in completely the wrong direction! The school secretary, who was on her way back from the bank, recognised the child and quickly took him back to school. Mr Prince had no idea that the child had spoken to him or that he had climbed over the gate. In fact, Mr Prince was not at all bothered about any of it.

Sometimes Mr Prince forgot the children's names, he regularly called Gemma 'Angela', and when she corrected him he said 'mm' and lifted his eyebrows like he didn't believe her.

Gemma was in a two-form entry school and the other Year 5 teacher was Mrs Turnpike. She remembered laughing out loud at that silly name.

Who would prefer to be with a teacher called Mrs Turnpike when you could be with a prince?, she thought. However, Mrs Turnpike turned out to be a beautifully attractive woman who always wore wonderful clothes and polished her nails. She had beautiful teeth and a huge sense of fun. The children in her class loved her and brought her gifts.

Both Mrs Turnpike and Mr Prince taught the same subjects at the same time, but in a very different way. Mrs Turnpike would dance around the classroom using any excuse to play music, while Mr Prince made the children work in silence and was not bothered if they were interested in the lessons or not. In maths, Mrs Turnpike marched the children around the playground singing prime numbers, while Mr Prince told children to learn them themselves in silence. In science, Mrs Turnpike set up elaborate experiments so that the children could be real scientists, while Mr Prince sometimes showed the children pictures, or a video if they were lucky.

In keeping with the teachers' names theory, Gemma remembered being scared of Mr Frazor, the caretaker; his name reminded her of a razor, all sharp and cutty. She hated watching her dad shave and thought it looked like it should hurt. But, Mr Frazor was a pussycat; he smiled and waved to all the children in the mornings, he knew all of their names and often let them help him with jobs around the school.

During the last lesson of the day, Mr Frazor popped into Gemma's classroom to replace a light bulb, so she asked Mr Prince if she could chat to Mr Frazor while he was working. As Gemma could have predicted, Mr Prince continued reading whatever it was he was reading, and just said 'mm'.

Apparently, Mr Frazor was an expert crocheter and was very happy to help Gemma with her nose–shaped shape. Gemma quickly sketched her design onto some scrap paper, as she hadn't brought her original drawing into school. Mr Frazor told her that they could probably get it done during a lunchtime one day. Seizing her opportunity, and of course the favourable snowy weather conditions, she asked Mr Frazor if she could find him the following day to learn how to crochet. Mr Frazor agreed, and told her that she would be able to find him snoozing in the storeroom. He followed this with 'Sshhhhh, don't tell anyone else,' and smiled broadly at her. They finished their conversation and Gemma sat back down to her very boring World War II worksheet.

Just before Mr Frazor left the room, he whispered to Gemma to remember her wool tomorrow. He smiled broadly again, picked up his ladder and tapped the side of his nose. Gemma smiled back; she liked Mr Frazor and decided that names could be deceptive. She could hear Mrs Turnpike next door, playing an exciting World War II video on the interactive whiteboard. The children in her class were going 'oooooohhh' and 'aaaaaahh' as they went on some kind of magical educational journey. Mr Prince stared into space while picking his yellow teeth and waiting for the afternoon to be over.

Gemma tried not to think about what she might be missing next door and decided to focus on 0.3 and Project Baldy. If she saw Greg on the way home she would arrange to go and check out Baldy's progress.

*

Gemma arrived at Greg's house and thought that Baldy must be using his indoor basket to snooze in - after all, there was snow on the ground and he did live a millionaire dog lifestyle. Greg's dad answered the door and invited her in.

'GREGGGG, Gemma's here. You alright, love? You look freezing, your cute little nose looks like it's about to drop off, ahh bless,' said Greg's dad.

Gemma begrudgingly squeezed out a very polite smile and a tiny nod. She really wanted to ignore him because of the nose comment, but she was far too well-mannered to actually be so rude. Greg began walking down the stairs, looking more dishevelled than usual. Apparently, Greg and Baldy had been working on the dog assault course and obedience skills since Greg had come home from school. He looked exhausted and unhappy, and there was no sign of Baldy anywhere.

'Hi, Greg, where's Baldy?' asked Gemma, concerned.

'He's left home,' replied Greg quietly.

'What? Can a dog leave home?' asked Gemma, a little shocked.

'Apparently they can; he's gone to live next door.

Mum says it's because I'm pushing him too hard.' Greg explained that following their training session, Baldy had walked out of the front door and into the garden next door. He'd scratched at his neighbour's door like a cat until they answered it, and then sauntered into the house. Greg's mum had followed Baldy to bring him back home, but she had been unsuccessful. She tried to pick him up, but as she touched him, he growled to warn her not to try! Baldy curled up in next door's cat's basket, closed his eyes and ignored her. She went back an hour later to find Baldy with next door's cat, Seafa, snuggled up together in what appeared to be a beautiful deep sleep. Greg went to look for himself - he patted Baldy and asked him to come home, but Baldy ignored him and continued with his nap.

'He's very comfortable next door; I'm worried that he won't want to come back home ever. He loves Seafa. I didn't think cats and dogs were supposed to get along, but those two will be getting married or something soon,' said Greg who was obviously very irritated by the cat-dog relationship thing. 'I feel really bad that I worked him so hard that he left home. I was only trying to help him to win the trophy.'

'What kind of training have you been doing?' asked Gemma quietly, whilst trying to imagine what could possibly have lead to Baldy's decision to leave home.

'Well,' replied Greg hesitantly. 'He wouldn't get up the ramp or through the hoop himself, so I put his lead on and kind of, erm, kind of, erm, kind of,' Greg's voice trailed off.

'Did you pull him up the see-saw?' Gemma asked, smiling to herself. The idea of Greg tugging at Baldy's lead to get him up the home-made see-saw was most amusing to her. As Gemma began to chuckle, a small smile began to creep across Greg's face. He knew he shouldn't have tugged on Baldy's lead to get him up the see-saw but he wanted to win that trophy so badly.

'He was quite good at balancing - he could do it by himself if he wanted to,' said Greg enthusiastically.

'So, we need to give him a reason to do it himself then,' replied Gemma. She was always the problem solver.

'If he ever decides to come back home,' replied Greg sadly.

Chapter 4

Mission Get Baldy Back

Gemma and Greg sat next to Baldy's empty basket, trying to think of a way to encourage him back home. They decided to write a list of all the things that Baldy liked, to see if they could perhaps entice him with any of them.

> THINGS THAT BALDY LIKES
> 1 FOOD
> 2 SLEEP
> 3 SEAFA

'Really, is that all he likes? Doesn't he like having a bath, or going for a walk, or chasing cats, oh, scratch that one, or, erm, I don't know, burying bones?'

'No, he doesn't really enjoy doing anything that involves moving,' replied Greg despondently.

'OK, so let's see what we can do with the list that we've got then,' chirped up Gemma. She hated seeing her friend so miserable and this made her quite determined to find a solution.

As Gemma read the list out loud, she quickly began to realise that Baldy had absolutely no reason to come back home. Seafa happily shared her cat food with him, and the neighbours always put extra food out for Baldy, which is why he'd decided to visit them in the first place, so number 1 on the list was covered. Numbers 2 and 3 were clearly well covered, as Baldy was currently comfortably cuddled up with the love of his life, snoring his fat head off! Gemma was trying to remain cheery for Greg's sake, and thinking hard about what would bring Baldy home. How could they get him back?

Greg and Gemma spent the next half an hour discussing ideas of how to get Baldy back. One bad idea lead to another until eventually Gemma jumped to her feet.

'Ahhhhh, I have it. There is one thing that Baldy can't get next door! It's you, Greg, he can't have you there! He loves Seafa, but he also loves you too - he'll miss you if he can't see you and this will help to bring him home!' A plan for Mission Get Baldy Back was underway.

Everyone knows that for a mission to run smoothly, it has to be planned to the last detail, so while Greg had been busily talking about what he thought they should do, Gemma being Gemma, and ultra-efficient, had used the opposite side of the THINGS BALDY LIKES paper to write step-by-step instructions for Mission Get Baldy Back.

MISSION GET BALDY BACK

1. Baldy must not see Greg at all. Even if this means that Greg has to wear a disguise when leaving the house – he must remain undetected!
2. The neighbours must not feed Seafa or Baldy.

(This may be tricky to negotiate, but Gemma thought that she might be able to pull these negotiations off as Greg had told her that when Baldy eats cat food his trumps smell like Sal's sandwiches. This was a bargaining tool that Gemma was very prepared to use. She reckoned it wouldn't be long before the cat food worked its way through Baldy's chubby gut, and he started to stink the neighbours out with his rotten smelly trumps.)

3. Hide Seafa's basket. (Again, there would need to be some negotiation with the neighbours about this, but Gemma was sure she could pull this off one way or another.)

4. Fill Baldy's shiny dinner bowl with his favourite food, and put a photo of Seafa next to the trophy picture, so he can see her without moving.

With all points planned in detail it was time to put Mission Get Baldy Back into operation immediately. Gemma needed thinking time. Greg's disguise had to be convincing.

Have you ever noticed how lazy people always find the easiest ways of doing things? This actually means that lazy people are really quite clever. This goes for lazy dogs too; it wasn't going to be easy to pull the wool over Baldy's eyes. Gemma was running over all kinds of ideas in her mind; maybe Greg should dress up as a girl, a footballer, an old man with grey hair and a moustache! They needed something that was Baldy-proof, something that would make Greg look completely different. Gemma could always be relied upon to come up with a good idea given time, so she sat and sat, and thought and thought, until eventually she was distracted.

DING DONG, DING DONG, sounded the front doorbell. Gemma walked into the hallway to get the door, but hesitated when she remembered that she wasn't in her own house. Greg's dad finally answered the door and Gemma stood by his side to see who the visitor was.

'Parcel for ya, mate,' came a deep voice from beneath the motorcycle courier's helmet. 'No need to sign for it, cheers,' shouted the courier, who swaggered off down the path and into the street.

'Oh, I wasn't expecting a delivery today,' said Greg's dad, smiling. He closed the front door and scurried off into the lounge to see what the mystery package contained.

Gemma walked back down the hallway towards the kitchen where she and Greg had been sitting. As she walked, her eyes were drawn to the kitchen window where she noticed something moving quickly though the garden. Was it Baldy coming home?

She took a closer look and there, standing in the middle of the lawn, hands on hips, staring directly at her, was the motorcycle courier! Gemma was quite puzzled and a little alarmed. She turned to fetch Greg's dad but she didn't need to, he was already walking towards her with his opened package and a piece of paper in his hands, mumbling and scratching his head.

'Well, you'd never guess what my delivery was!' He handed her a small piece of paper which read:

I am the parcel delivery man. Look, look closely, it's me, Greg!

As Gemma read the note, the motorcycle courier took off his helmet to reveal a very smiley Greg. He walked through the back door, into the kitchen and proudly announced, 'Point 1, sorted.' Gemma and Greg's dad both looked at him in amazement. The disguise was fabulous; he had made himself taller by wearing a pair of his mum's high-heeled boots underneath his dad's old boiler suit, and his face had been completely covered by the helmet.

'Brilliant, totally brilliant,' shouted Gemma, 'now all we need to do is test this disguise out on Baldy.'

'Well, I just delivered a parcel next door and he never batted an eyelid,' said Greg excitedly.

'Hmm, I'm not sure that proves anything; he usually ignores you!' said Gemma, smiling. 'Not even a tiny little tail wag?' she questioned.

'Nope, not even a twitch. I know he doesn't usually do what I tell him to do, but he always wags his tail when he sees me.'

'Oof, you kids, what are you up to now?' asked Greg's dad.

'Mission Get Baldy Back,' replied Greg and Gemma in unison.

'What did you put into the parcel that you delivered next door?' quizzed Greg's dad.

'I put a picture of the competition trophy inside, so that Baldy wouldn't forget how lovely it is,' said Greg proudly.

'Oh, you and that blooming competition. He's a dog, not a circus elephant, although he is nearly the size of an elephant,' chuckled Greg's dad as he walked back into the lounge to do a bit more of whatever it is that adults do in the lounge.

So, it was onto Point 2 of Mission Get Baldy Back and both Gemma and Greg decided it was best to leave this one until last. The neighbours would find it easier not to feed Baldy once they had actually experienced one of his trumps. Greg knew that if they waited a while, Baldy's trumps would be starting to brew very nicely, and he may have even let a few little smelly ones escape already.

Gemma was always in control of any operation that she and Greg decided to carry out. However, Greg had sorted Point 1 out before Gemma had even come up with a workable idea, and he was now swiftly moving onto Point 3. This took Gemma by surprise a bit, but when she thought about it, she decided it was quite nice to work with someone as enthusiastic as herself, and working through the list was really cheering Greg up, so she sat back a little and listened to his next plan.

'We need to sabotage the basket, Gem. I don't think hiding it will do the trick; it's too obvious and he's a very clever dog. We need to make it uncomfortable for Baldy and his girlfriend. We need to make it so uncomfortable that they can't sleep in it,' said Greg as he hung onto his chin, searching his brain for more ideas.

'I agree, we need him to want to come back home to his own comfy basket. Hmm ... hmm... ahh ha! ICE,' shouted Gemma. 'We should sneak some ice cubes in between the bottom of the basket and the cat blanket. To begin with the ice will be sharp and uncomfortable to lie on, like when you try to lie on a beach that has rocks hiding in the sand. Then it will be cold and uncomfortable, like when you hurt yourself at school and they make you stick frozen peas on yourself until your head goes numb. Why it has to be peas, I don't know! Finally, as the ice begins to melt it will be cold, wet and very uncomfortable, exactly what we want. What do you think?'

'Ohhh, poor Baldy, he'll hate that, poor dog. It's a fantastic idea!'

'Hahahahaha, I love it when a plan comes together,' giggled Gemma.

So, Gemma and Greg decided to leave it until a little later, when old whiffy bum was really starting to churn out the cat-food trumps, and Gemma would pop around next door to negotiate feeding strategies and sneak the ice cubes into the cat basket. Greg knew that the best time would be when Baldy was getting hungry. In around an hour's time, Baldy would get up out of his bed and start sniffing around for something to eat. Hopefully if there wasn't anything to munch, he'd lie back down for a while, but, if all went to plan, there would be an uncomfortable, cold surprise waiting for him in his bed. Greg checked the freezer to make sure there was plenty of ice ready, and of course there was; it was winter time. Have you ever noticed that there's always ice when you don't need it? There's just never any ice in the summer. Greg wondered to himself how that could work.

Chapter 5

Gemma the Thief!

Gemma prepared herself for Mission Get Baldy Back. She was armed with a carrier bag half full of ice cubes, and, to ensure that the mission was successful, she'd run through what she was going to say to Mr and Mrs Nextdoor in her head. She breathed in deeply and knocked on the door.

Mr Nextdoor opened the door, propped himself up with his walking stick and the door frame, and asked how he could help. Gemma explained that she was Greg's friend and told him that Greg was too upset to visit himself as he missed Baldy so much, and that she was there to try to help her friend get his dog back. Gemma estimated that Mr Nextdoor must be at least one hundred and forty years old, but he was very friendly and invited her in so that they could chat about Baldy. Mr Nextdoor then went on and on about how much he enjoyed having Baldy as a guest and Gemma began to worry that Mission Get Baldy Back, might be a little bit more tricky than she had first thought. It took Mr Nextdoor ages to get back to his chair; he was a frail old man with a poorly leg, who looked like a small version of Father Christmas without the red suit or the big belly.

'Now, chicken, what can we do about your dog?'

'Well, Mr... erm, erm...' Gemma suddenly realised

that she had no idea what Mr Nextdoor's real name was. Surely it wasn't Mr Nextdoor was it? 'Erm, like I said, Greg is really missing Baldy and he'd like him to come home as soon as possible Mr erm...' Gemma's voice trailed off.

'Did you hear something?' asked Mr Nextdoor, turning his head towards the door. Gemma had heard a faint noise while she was talking, but was determined to get Baldy back so had tried to ignore the interruption. *Paaaaaaarrrrrrrrp*, came the noise again as both Gemma and Mr Nextdoor listened intently. It wasn't long before they knew what the paaaaaaaarping noise had been. Gemma and Mr Nextdoor both covered their noses with their hands as the smell of cat-foody trump made its way into the lounge.

'Oh dear me, ohhhh dear me, please excuse Seafa, she doesn't usually do that, ohh dear, how very embarrassing,' apologised a now red-faced Mr Nextdoor.

'Ah, this is what I wanted to talk to you about, Mr erm...' Gemma was getting annoyed with herself now. Why did she keep forgetting that she didn't know his name and have to keep calling him Mr Erm? Moving swiftly on and trying not to call him, 'Mr Erm,' Gemma told Mr Erm that the smell was actually coming from Baldy and not Seafa. She explained that Baldy ate everything in sight and that the pungent smell that they were experiencing right now was the result of Baldy eating Seafa's dinner.

Paaaaaaarrrrrrrrp came the noise again, followed

33

by a shuffling sound from the kitchen. Mr Nextdoor sighed as he realised that he was soon to be gassed out again and Gemma asked if it was OK if she went to look at Baldy to make sure he was alright. She explained that Baldy might need a trip out into the garden to carry out some business. Mr Nextdoor, imagining what Baldy's business might look and smell like on his kitchen floor, quickly agreed and Gemma picked up her carrier bag and rushed off.

As Gemma reached the kitchen, the smell got thicker and thicker. Poor Baldy was standing as far away from Seafa's basket as he could, his nose was wrinkled up like there was a bad smell under it and he was looking particularly sorry for himself. Seafa was curled up by the back door with her nose tucked firmly under both of her paws.

Gemma knew that this was her opportunity to sabotage the basket. She had the basket in sight, the ice in her bag - it was time to go, go, go.

'Everything alright, chicken?' called Mr Nextdoor, who was making his way towards the kitchen to find out if he needed to hire some industrial cleaning services to deal with Baldy's business.

'Erm, erm, yes, yes, everything's fine,' stuttered Gemma, trying to sound cool as she wildly stuffed ice cubes into Seafa's basket. 'I'm just checking that the basket's clean,' she called, trying to buy herself a little more time.

'It might be a good idea to open the back door chicken, you know, to let the clean air in. It's a bit unbearable that smell, chick'.

'OK, yes, it is unbearable. The sooner Baldy goes home the better I think, don't you, Mr Erm?' Gemma growled at herself for doing the Mr Erm thing again.

'Yes, chicken, I think he needs to go to the vet; he's definitely not right in the tummy department,'

Ahhhh, 'job done,' sighed Gemma as she could see Mr Nextdoor's shadow approaching the door. She picked up her empty carrier bag to hide all evidence and suddenly realised that she couldn't explain why her bag was now empty if Mr Nextdoor asked. *Aaaaarrrrrrgggghhhhhhh.* In panic, she scanned the kitchen for something to put into her bag to make it look as full as it had done when she arrived. *Bananas NO, plates NO, chair, oh come on Gemma, think, think, Seafa aaarggh no stupid girl, erm, erm...* Gemma saw Mr Nextdoor's hand appear on the door frame and grabbed the closest thing to her that would fit in the bag. She quickly shoved a pile of 'something' into her bag as Mr Nextdoor's walking stick made its snail-like way into the kitchen, followed by his smiley Father Christmas face.

'Ere you are, chicken, here's the key for the back door.' Mr Nextdoor handed Gemma the key while he used his hand to waft Baldy's bum smell from under his nose. Trying to look very calm, Gemma took the key and opened the back door. Both Baldy and Seafa trotted out and filled their lungs with the fresh air.

'Mr erm...' Gemma actually growled out loud at herself this time. 'Please may I ask you a favour?'

'Of course, chicken, what can I do for you?' replied Mr Nextdoor most agreeably.

'Because Baldy keeps eating Seafa's dinner, and it's clearly not good for him, could you stop putting Seafa's cat food out for her until Baldy decides to come home? He loves cat food as much as he loves, well, any food, but the smell situation will only get worse if he keeps swallowing it down like a gannet.'

'Hmmmm,' said Mr Nextdoor, rubbing his fluffy white beard. 'How long do you think it'll be before he decides to go home, chick? I can't starve poor Seafa, but I have to admit that I would find it hard to live with that smell. I do love having Baldy here, but ewwwwww, that pong.'

'It won't be long; Greg's filled his bowl with dog food and he'll be back when he's hungry, maybe an hour or two. Maybe you could give Seafa little treats without Baldy seeing just for the next couple of hours?' suggested Gemma.

'Alright, chick, I can do that. Shall we just see if Baldy wants to go back next door with you now?'

suggested Mr Nextdoor. The smell was really very bad, and he didn't want to starve Seafa, so this might be a better solution all round.

'I'll give it a go,' said Gemma, knowing full well that Baldy would pretend that he couldn't see or hear her. She walked out into the garden and called Baldy a few times. As predicted he lay side by side with Seafa, basking in the winter sunshine and ignoring her completely. She put her hand on his collar and gave it a little, tiny tug. He opened one eye, growled softly until she let go and then calmly closed his eye. Gemma hadn't forgotten about when Baldy had bitten her and he hadn't forgotten either! He knew that she was scared of him and knew that all he needed to do was growl a little to get his own way. The truth was that deep down, Baldy was sad that he'd bitten Gemma; he was only a puppy and she'd scared him. However, he was also a little bit envious of her friendship with Greg. Baldy wanted to be Greg's best friend and sometimes Gemma got in the way. When this happened, he thought that she had deserved her bite.

'I don't think he's quite ready yet.' Gemma was so pleased with herself for not doing the Mr Erm thing that she smiled to herself as she made her way back to the kitchen. 'Thank you, I'll just go and check that Baldy's dinner bowl's full. I'm sure he'll smell it and come to get it soon.'

'Alright, chicken, I won't feed Seafa until Baldy's gone.'

Gemma made her way to the front door, leaving Mr

Nextdoor perched on a kitchen stool.

'Chicken,' called out Mr Nextdoor as Gemma was about to leave. She turned to listen to him. 'My name is Mr Langry, but most people call me Santa cuz of the beard.' A broad smile filled his face.

'My name is Gemma,' replied Gemma smiling back, 'although most people call me chick because they can't remember it.' Gemma smiled and waved to Santa as she left, feeling very pleased with having completed Points 2 and 3 of Mission Get Baldy Back.

Chapter 6

Photo Shoot

Gemma stood at Greg's doorstep for ages. She rang and rang the bell, but no one answered. She walked around the back of the house and into the garden. There she found the motorcycle courier figure, aka Greg, standing on top of a step ladder, wearing high-heeled boots, dangling precariously over next door's fence.

'What on earth are you up to?'

'I'm getting a photo of Seafa,' announced Greg in his big motorcycle courier voice.

'Oh, I see, she's just on the decking - can you see her?'

'Just about, I just need to move a tiny little bit to the   RIIIIIIGGGGGGHHHHHHHTTTTTTTT,' screeched Greg as the ladder tipped very slowly, making him fall head first into an overgrown conifer tree. Gemma found this hilarious and couldn't help Greg to get out of the tree because she was laughing so much. Eventually, she caught her breath, reached one of his legs and tugged him so that he could free himself. Greg clambered out of the conifer and Gemma lifted the visor of his helmet to see if he was alright.

Greg's smile was as broad as ever. 'I want to do that again!'

'I want to see you do that again, it was hilarious,' giggled Gemma.

Gemma held the bottom of the step ladder while Greg took the photo of Seafa, this time without falling off the ladder and landing head-first in the conifer. They downloaded it to Greg's laptop and printed it out. Seafa's picture looked very cute by the trophy picture above Baldy's overfull feeding bowl. Now, the children needed to sit it out and wait for Baldy to return. They waited and waited but Baldy didn't come back.

Chapter 7

Gemma the Unthief

There is nothing more thrilling than opening the curtains to find yet more snow. No matter what day of the week, Gemma was always excited to see snow. However, today it was super exciting because it was Saturday, which meant that she could play out in it all day. This made Gemma instantly think about Nose Warmer 0.3. She hadn't given 0.3 much thought since Mission Get Baldy Back had started. She searched out the lovely pink wool from the bottom of her wardrobe and put it into her school bag ready for her hush-hush lunchtime meeting on Monday with Mr Frazor. Sitting next to her school bag, Gemma noticed the ice carrier bag, and decided to look inside to see what it was that she had stuffed into it yesterday.

'Oh my goodness, ohhhhh my goodness!' whispered Gemma to herself as she pulled pair after pair of Mr Langry's pants out of the carrier bag. Of all the things that she could have stuffed into the bag, why did it have to be pants? *Ewwwwww,* thought Gemma, *are they clean or dirty?* The pants were in a neat pile, one on top of the other and all the right way round. Gemma thought that no one would neatly stack their dirty pants before they went into the washing machine, so she concluded that they must be clean, *pheeeeeew.*

She also realised that she needed to return Mr Langry's pants ASAP, before he noticed that they were missing! Imagine trying to explain to anyone that you'd stolen lots of pairs of Santa's pants! Getting dressed as quickly as she could, Gemma left the house and began trudging through the soft, newly fallen snow to Greg's house. For today, Gemma had to make do with the wet-breath-scarf solution to keep her nose pink. It wasn't ideal but she couldn't crochet yet, so it was better than nothing. While walking, Gemma was desperately trying to think of a way of returning Santa's pants without being detected. Should she climb over Greg's fence and then climb in through the kitchen window? *No, she thought, that probably wouldn't work, it's too cold to have the windows open today.* Could she use the motorcycle courier to deliver them for her? No, Santa was bound to have realised that this was Greg by now. Should she put them by Santa's door step, knock on the door and run away? No, not a good idea; Santa often sat in the window people-watching. He might see her and that would make things even more awkward. Gemma was running out of time and out of ideas!

As she turned the corner into Greg's road, Gemma was really pleased to see that the newsagent's shop light was on. She'd been in such a rush that she'd skipped breakfast and was starving now. She wondered if Seafa had had anything to eat yet, and then wondered if Baldy had gone back home. Inside the shop, Gemma picked up a packet of crisps and a chocolate bar. She knew it wasn't a healthy breakfast, but it was exceptional circumstances so it didn't matter once in a while. Besides, crisps are made from potatoes so she reckoned that she could count them as one of her five a day. On the way to the till she checked out the special offers. She often shopped with her mum, who was a super bargain buyer.

SPECIAL OFFERS
Nappies, half price – not interested.
Biscuits, a third off, tempting but still a bit pricey.
Soup, buy one get one free – not interested, but why don't they just sell them at half price like the nappies?
Bleach, buy two get one free – not interested. What do people use that for and why would you ever want three of them?
Cat food, reduced to 20p a tin, out of date this month – not interested, don't have a cat – ohhhhhh, but Santa does and Baldy had eaten Seafa's so it would only be polite to replace it. This was Gemma's way back into the house! If she kindly delivered Seafa some replacement cat food, she might also be able to return Santa's pants.

Armed with half a packet of crisps, a chocolate bar and two tins of cat food - well, who wouldn't buy two at that price? Gemma arrived at Greg's house. *DING DONG* went the tacky electronic door bell... *DING DONG*. She rang it again. Finally, Greg's dad answered the door wearing his dressing gown.

'Is that you, Gemma?' he asked quizzically. 'I can barely see you under that thick scarf.'

43

'Hi, yes, it's me. Is Greg in please? I have something I need to talk to him about.'

Greg's dad stood to the side and motioned with his arm for Gemma to come in.

'Thank you,' said Gemma as she began to peel away all of the layers that she was wearing to keep the cold out, all except for the scarf, of course. Gemma was eagerly searching to see if she could see any sign of Baldy, but she could see nothing to make her think that he was home. Greg came creeping down the stairs, doing that fingers on lips thing that teachers make you do when you're in nursery. Gemma didn't think that she was being particularly noisy taking off her coat, but she complied anyway.

'Hi, Gem, you alright?' mouthed Greg.

'Erm, I have a problem I need to talk to you about please, in private,' whispered Gemma.

'Let's go into the kitchen. He's asleep in my bed so we can't go in there; I don't want to wake him, he's had a terrible night,' said Greg shaking his head.

'Who's asleep in your bed? I've just seen your dad - he looks perfectly fine to me'.

'Nooooo, not Dad, Baldy! Baldy's asleep in my bed; he was howling in the middle of the night at the front door.

'Oh wow, that's fantastic news. Did our plan work?' asked Gemma.

'He was sooooo cold his little nose was like an icicle. Speaking of which, have you forgotten to take your scarf off, or is there some kind of new fashion that makes you wear crisps attached to a scarf round your chin?'

Gemma was well aware that she was still wearing her scarf, but she hadn't realised that she'd got bits of her crisps stuck to it. She carefully unwrapped her nose and, using the microwave as a mirror, mentally scored it as a nine out of ten on the pinkness scale. Then she began to pick away at the bits of crisps stuck to her scarf. *All the more reason to crack on with 0.3,* she thought to herself. She would have no problem at all eating crisps with her new design.

'So, what's the secret?' asked Greg excitedly.

'You will never guess what I have in this carrier bag, never in a million years!' said Gemma playfully.

'Hmm, let me think, let me think.' Greg was craning his neck to try to peek a look inside the bag, but even if he did sneak a peek, he still probably couldn't have guessed what he was looking at. 'Is it something to help me to train Baldy with?' he asked hopefully. The idea of Greg using Santa's pants to train Baldy made Gemma laugh.

'No, Greg, definitely not,' said Gemma, still chuckling to herself.

'Is it something to eat?'

'Erm, yes in a way,' said Gemma remembering that there were pants and cat food in the bag.

'OK, now, listen carefully and stop me when I get it,' said Greg, breathing in very deeply.

'Is it: fish, faggots, fried chicken, biscuits, bananas, beans, broccoli, beefburgers, carrots, cucumber, cannelloni, cabbage, potatoes, plums, pork pies, pickle, pasties? he enquired hopefully.

'Nope, not even close.'

'Hmm, OK, let's have another go at this then,' mumbled Greg. He then proceeded to walk around, saying everything that he could see. 'Is it: a magazine, a small table, a clock, a coaster, a handbag, a photograph, a telephone, a pen, a lamp or a ball?' he asked, looking to see Gemma's reactions to each of his suggestions.

Gemma shook her head as he reeled off his list.

'You'll never guess,' giggled Gemma. 'Do you give up yet?'

'Nooooo, I don't give up! OK, so, is it something you find in a kitchen?' This question made Gemma roar with laughter; she had to answer yes, because that's exactly where she had found Santa's pants, but in being truthful, she knew she wasn't helping Greg at all.

'Shhhhhhhh, you'll wake Baldy, he needs his sleep. He tried really hard to nap on that ice-filled bed you made for him. In fact, he tried so hard he nearly caught hypothermia!'

'You mean, he's so lazy, he couldn't be bothered to move until he thought he might die!' commented Gemma.

'OK, so, is it … a kettle, eggs, coffee, apples, bananas, nuts, book, matches, cake, smelly candle thing, fluffy rat, teapot, ornament, sharp knife, salt or pepper?'

Gemma continued to shake her head whilst pointing out that Greg might now be disqualified from the guessing game as he'd said 'bananas' twice.

Through her giggles, Gemma asked, 'Why do you have a fluffy rat in the kitchen? Is that normal?'

'It is in our house,' replied Greg without giving any further explanation. 'You're right, I can't guess,' he said, pleased with himself for having had a good go, though.

'Well, I'll have to tell you then. I have a bag full of Mr Langry's pants!' she announced proudly.

'What, who's Mr Langry?'

'He's your next door neighbour!' exclaimed Gemma.

'Oh, you mean Santa. What, why on earth do you have Santa's pants in your bag?' asked Greg, most bewildered by what he was hearing. Gemma explained about the empty ice bag problem, and Greg thought that she'd been pretty smart to think of refilling the bag. He was quite sure that he wouldn't have considered it at all. Greg was often impressed by Gemma's geeky kind of coolness. She wasn't cool like the trendy kids, but she was cleverly cool and he secretly wished he could be more like her. Gemma went on to explain about her cat food idea, giving Greg all the details to see if he thought it would work.

*

So, once again, Gemma found herself ringing Mr Nextdoor's bell. Like before, she had pre-rehearsed what she was going to say. The only difference was that this time Greg was with her, and she hoped that this might make it a little easier.

'Morning, Santa,' Gemma chirped up cheerily. She really liked Santa even though his surname suggested that she might not.

'Ah, morning chicken, our plan to get your dog back worked eventually,' Santa smiled. 'He was doing some howling in the night though, Greg.' Santa lifted his eyebrows as he tutted in Greg's direction.

'As a thank you, and to replace what Baldy ate, we bought some cat food for Seafa,' said Greg as sweetly as he could manage.

'Oh, how kind of you. She's sleeping at the moment, it was a bit of a busy night with one thing and another, but I'll give it to her when she wakes up.' Santa reached out his hand to collect the cat food and this was when Gemma had to make her move.

'Here you go,' sang Gemma as she squeezed past Santa, through the door and into the hallway. 'I'll put it in the kitchen for you so that you don't have to struggle with walking and carrying it.' Before he could agree, Gemma was in the kitchen unpacking the cat food and the pants. She arrived back at the door within moments, and although he was a little shocked by Gemma inviting herself into his house, Santa thanked her and remarked at how thoughtful she was.

'Greg,' called Santa as the children were beginning

to walk down the path. 'You really do need to take Baldy to the vet, he's got terrible tummy trouble. He did the most enormous wee in Seafa's basket - the poor girl nearly drowned. I know you've house trained him properly because he's never done that before, so you really should get him checked out. Oh, before you go, one more thing, please could you ask your mum if she'll put this into her tumble dryer for me? It's Seafa's blanket. I had to wash it and it's too cold for it to dry outside. She struggles to sleep without it, she's a snuggly little kitty. Do you think your mum would mind?'

Greg ran back up the path to collect the blanket. He was quite sure his mum wouldn't mind; she often helped Santa out when Mrs Santa wasn't around. This reminded Greg that he hadn't seen Mrs Santa for a while, so he quickly asked how she was.

'She's a poor old dear now, Greg, we both are,' replied Santa with a faint smile. 'She's been in hospital for over a week - she's struggling to shift a cold that she's had. I'm going to see her tonight if the snow doesn't come down any more. I've got lots to tell her about Baldy and Seafa; she loves to catch up on the gossip.'

'I'll let Mum know that she's in hospital. Send her our best,' said Greg, although he had no idea what that meant. It was just something he'd heard people saying when they knew someone was ill.

Greg and Gemma chuckled to themselves as they walked down the path. The idea that Baldy had done a massive, icy wee in poor Seafa's basket made both of them laugh out loud. Indeed, if Baldy really was doing wees that big and that cold, he really should visit the vet immediately!

Greg's mum put Seafa's blanket into the tumble dryer, while Gemma and Greg chatted and laughed about their adventures on Mission Get Baldy Back to date.

So far they had managed to:

1. Sneak ice cubes into the neighbour's cat basket
2. Take secret photos of his cat
3. Steal his pants
4. Return his pants

...and all without being detected.

While they chatted, Baldy slowly made his way down the stairs. He passed his food bowl without even a sniff, and trotted off towards the back door.

'Alright now, lad?' asked Greg, as Baldy walked blindly past him, ignoring him as usual. 'I wonder where he's off to?' Better check that he doesn't actually need to do some business. I'll open the back door for him, back in a min,' called Greg, who was already nearly at the kitchen door. Within seconds, Greg came stumbling back towards Gemma, clutching his stomach - he looked like he was in awful pain.

'What's up, what have you done?'

Greg straightened up a little and Gemma could immediately see that he wasn't in pain at all - he was actually crying with laughter, and he could barely speak. He motioned that Gemma should follow him into the utility room. Seconds later, Gemma was also crying with laughter as she watched Baldy sitting in front of the tumble dryer, captivated by Seafa's blanket going round and round and round. It was pure comedy watching the silly dog's head copying the circles made by the machine, his eyes unblinking and his tongue hanging out. Greg patted Baldy's head but there was no response. He put his food bowl by the tumble dryer; still no reaction. He was completely transfixed.

Chapter 8

Baldy's Workout

So, it was time to begin dog training again. Even though there was snow on the ground, the training had to be relentless. There was no time to waste; the competition was looming. Baldy had recovered from his freezing-wee-and-cat-food-trump extravaganza and he was lazily settled back in at home. Greg thought it better not to put Baldy's lead on him for training, just in case he was tempted to 'help' him up the see-saw again. The garden was already laid out as a dog assault course and Greg was ready to begin. Baldy, however, was snuggled up in his basket snoozing the day away as usual. Greg had tried very hard to limit Baldy's food supply, but he had to admit that he was concerned that if he didn't feed him regularly enough, he would leave home and go to live with Seafa again.

It was about half an hour before dinner time, and Greg decided to try an experiment. He got one spoonful of dog food, put it into Baldy's feeding bowl and placed it at the end of the assault course, at the bottom of the garden. Baldy was there like a shot, and he'd eaten it before Greg had had a chance to take the spoon out of the bowl. Greg had never seen him move so fast!

This gave Greg another idea. This time he put the

empty bowl on the floor just beyond the see-saw. He also put the picture of the trophy by the bowl and told Baldy that to get the food he had to climb the see-saw. Baldy sniffed around the bowl, saw there was nothing in it, and began to walk inside the house. Greg then had his best idea of all. He put a small spoon of dog food halfway up the see-saw; it was just out of Baldy's reach. The only way that Baldy could get the food was to climb onto the see-saw. As Baldy smelt the food, he raced towards the see-saw, stopped, sniffed and gingerly put his two front paws onto the plank of wood. Very carefully, he made his way to the food and balanced beautifully while he gobbled it up.

Quickly realising that he needed Baldy to complete the whole see-saw, Greg put another spoon of food into his bowl, and Baldy gracefully walked down the other side of the see-saw to fill his face. Greg was elated. He patted and stroked his dog and showed him the trophy again, just to be sure that he understood how important it was. As usual, Baldy looked unimpressed.

Greg decided that this was definitely the way to inspire Baldy to become an active and obedient dog. He was just trying to fathom out a way of getting Baldy to jump over the small dog jump that he'd made, when Seafa trotted daintily into the garden. Baldy immediately ran through Greg's home made tunnel and easily over the dog jump. He obliterated the slalom section of the course to arrive at Seafa's side to nuzzle her nose in a kind of kissing action. Greg didn't know whether to be happy or throw up.

Baldy was clearly very capable of completing the assault course, so there was still a chance that he could win that beautiful trophy, but this cat-dog relationship thing really was very sickly. There was absolutely no chance, now that Little Miss Wonderful had arrived, that Baldy would do anything for Greg.

He left the nauseating lovers together and went inside for dinner. He giggled at the idea that his mum might use his motivational strategy on him. He imagined her standing with his dinner, saying, 'put that book away and then you can have a spoonful. Now put your shoes away and you can have another.' He thought he might do this to his children when he was a grown-up, it's much more fun than nagging. But then he quickly remembered that having children might involve kissing, so there was clearly no reason at all for him to remember this technique, other than for him to use on Baldy, of course.

*

The following few days saw a similar training programme for Baldy. He climbed things and jumped over things for spoonfuls of food; he'd soon realised that the only way he would get fed, was if he performed like a circus elephant. Sometimes Greg got annoyed when Seafa interrupted their training. He always tried to separate them because the competition was getting closer and closer, and time was running out. But Baldy appeared to be blissfully happy when he was with her, and Greg was careful to keep him happy.

Now that he knew that Baldy could complete the course, he needed to encourage him to do it without the food. He tried putting his full bowl at the end of the course, but Baldy still ran the entire length of the garden without stopping to jump, or go through his hoop, and simply filled his face. Now Greg had to leave it a while before he continued training, as Baldy wasn't hungry any more. Greg despondently shuffled up to his bedroom, and gazed through the window. Baldy was snoozing happily at the top of the garden. There were only three days left until the competition, and he was wondering whether he should give up. He sat on his bed and imagined how good the trophy would look on his windowsill. Hopefully this would help him to regain his enthusiasm. Surely there must be some way of encouraging Baldy to compete without food?

Chapter 9

Oops, Neeee Naaaaaw Neeeeee

Naaaaaw

Gemma was disappointed with progress on 0.3. In fact, she hadn't made any progress at all. Mr Frazor had been off school sick for a few days and she was beginning to wonder if she should make him a get well soon card. Sal said that her mum might be able to help Gemma with crocheting, but Gemma really wanted Mr Frazor to help because he was kind and reliable. Sal's mum was a little bit wacky and would probably mix up knitting with crocheting and embroidering and sewing. She seemed to pay no attention to details at all. Sometimes Sal would wear odd shoes, or a bikini under her clothes instead of underwear. It was definitely unusual, but Sal would say, 'Does it really matter as long as you're clean and warm?' Gemma couldn't decide if this was OK or not.

Gemma regularly thought about the most obscure things, like why businessmen wear ties. Does it help them to do their important jobs better? Does it keep their necks warm? Is it for catching bits of dinner that they drop like a baby's bib? She wondered why people fanned their face with their hands when they were about to cry, like they can somehow wave the tears away. She also wondered why her mum insisted that she wear her massive duffel coat on foggy mornings. In Gemma's experience, foggy mornings always brought sunny days, so she would be boiling on the way home from school with her duffel coat on.

However, today Gemma was excited about wearing new wellies to school. She'd been dying for her mum to order them online, and finally they'd arrived. They were light blue and had pictures of snowmen and snowballs on them. In contrast to Gemma's brand new wellies, Sal had arrived wearing a pair of trainers with carrier bags over the top of them to keep them dry. She'd put elastic bands around the tops of the bags to keep them up, and that seemed to work quite well. There was one tiny little design fault with them though; they were ridiculously slippy. She'd fallen over twice in five minutes, and the more she tried not to slip, the more difficulty she seemed to encounter. When Sal noticed Gemma in the playground, she was very excited about some news that she wanted to share. She started to run towards Gemma, but the carrier bag wellies struck again! Sal's feet slipped from underneath her, she fell backwards and bumped her head very hard on the snowy playground. Gemma ran to help her, but Sal was lying on the ground motionless.

'Sal, Sal,' called Gemma. Sal didn't move. 'Miss, Miss, please come and help, Sal's in trouble,' she shouted to the teacher who was on playground duty.

Mrs Turnpike came running over to see what the problem was. She took one look at Sal, took her phone out of her pocket and called 999. While she was asking for an ambulance, she sent a child to fetch the head teacher. She took her coat off and carefully placed it over Sal, and told her it was to keep her warm. Gemma began to get upset, and Mrs Turnpike told her to hold Sal's hand and to talk to her.

'What shall I talk to her about, Miss?' questioned Gemma who had huge tears in her eyes.

'Tell her about what you did on holiday or something, sweetie, just keep talking to her, it will help her.'

Mrs Turnpike asked Gemma how Sal had fallen, how she had landed, and if she had bumped her head. Gemma described what had happened and both Mrs Turnpike and Mrs Dainty listened and thanked her.

*

Within a couple of minutes an ambulance arrived. Lots of children had gathered round now to see what the fuss was about, and Mrs Dainty was busily shooing them away to their classes. Mrs Turnpike talked to the ambulance men and gave them all of the information that she had gathered about Sal's fall.

'Fetch the stretcher, please, John,' called the ambulance man to the driver.

Gemma's mind began racing; what part of Sal needed to be stretched? How could stretching her help her at all?

'Mrs Turnpike,' said Gemma in a very worried

voice. 'Why do they want to stretch Sal?'

'Sorry, sweetie, what do you mean?' quizzed Mrs Turnpike.

'The ambulance man said that he needed the driver to fetch a stretcher. What are they going to stretch?' asked Gemma, who was now very concerned.

'Oh, I see,' said Mrs Turnpike, smiling. 'A stretcher is that kind of bed on wheels there, look, they're bringing it now.'

Gemma was so relieved but couldn't help wondering why it was called a stretcher and not a bed on wheels. Sal was gently put onto the stretcher. As she was moved, she opened her eyes and said, 'Gemma.'

Gemma squeezed her hand to let her know that she had heard her and said, 'It's OK, Sal, I'm here.'

'What's happening?' asked Sal in a frightened voice. One of the ambulance men came to Sal's side and asked her what her name was and her birthday. He then looked at Mrs Turnpike, who nodded to confirm that what Sal had said was correct. The ambulance man held Sal's other hand and explained to her that he was going to take her to hospital.

'Stay with me please, Gemma, I don't want to go by myself.' Sal looked at the ambulance man to see if he would let Gemma go with her. The ambulance man looked at Mrs Turnpike, and Mrs Turnpike looked at Mrs Dainty.

'I need to get parental approval to allow a child out of school,' said Mrs Dainty, in her most official voice. Mrs Turnpike immediately telephoned the school office, and asked them to phone Gemma's mum for approval. She was far more efficient than Mrs Dainty, who really hadn't got to grips with mobile phones or computers yet. Gemma continued to hold Sal's hand while she was transported on her magic wheelie bed, into the back of the ambulance.

'Would you like to go with Sal, Gemma?' asked Mrs Turnpike as she popped her head around the ambulance door.

'Yes please, if I'm allowed,' replied Gemma, instantly feeling Sal's hand relax in hers.

'OK, sweetie, your mum says it's fine for you to go, and I'm going to come with you too.' Both girls loved Mrs Turnpike, and were very relieved that she was going with them instead of Mrs Dainty.

'Alright, Sal love, I need to ask you a couple of questions, OK, poppet?' said the ambulance man in a singy-songy kind of voice.

'OK,' replied Sal.

The ambulance man asked lots and lots of questions. He asked Sal to count to twenty, then how many fingers he was holding up, followed by 'What day is it today?' Sal commented that the questions were very easy and wished maths tests were as simple.

'So, poppet, do you have any pain anywhere, love?'

'Yes, my head hurts at the back, it's throbbing like it did when I got hit with a hockey ball,' replied Sal.

'OK, poppet, let me take a look.' The ambulance man leaned Sal forward, while he carefully inspected the back of her head. 'Hmmm, you must have gone with a right bump, you've got a nasty lump there, love.'

'I was running to tell Gemma some news but I slipped and... well, I don't remember anything else,' said Sal.

Gemma, still holding Sal's hand, was looking around the inside of the ambulance. She'd never been in an ambulance before. There was lots to read and loads and loads of equipment all in little boxes attached to the walls. She found it odd that she could see perfectly out of the windows, but that no one on the outside could see in. It made her want to pull funny faces at the people standing to cross at the traffic lights, but this was a serious situation so she thought she'd better not. She was also desperately waiting for the ambulance man to stop talking so that she could ask Sal what the exciting news was.

Mrs Turnpike was busy talking to Sal's mum on her mobile, giving her all the details of what had happened so far, and telling her which hospital to go to.

The ambulance man continued to ask questions while he looked at Sal's hands and then shone a torch into her eyes.

'What did you have for breakfast this morning, love?'

'Beef risotto and strawberries,' replied Sal.

'No, poppet, not dinner last night, I mean breakfast this morning. Have you had any breakfast today, love?' enquired the ambulance man, who was quite sure that Sal was mixed up.

'Yes, I had beef risotto and strawberries,' repeated Sal, not really understanding why he had asked the same question twice. The ambulance man looked at

Gemma because Mrs Turnpike was still gassing to Sal's mum.

'Erm, she does have some, well, erm...' Gemma didn't want to offend Sal by saying, 'odd things to eat', so instead she said 'different meals'. Sal's breakfast was a revelation to Gemma; she'd only known that she had odd sandwiches, but now she knew that she had odd breakfasts too.

*

By the time they arrived at hospital, Sal had been thoroughly checked over by the ambulance man and was sitting upright on the magic wheelie bed. She seemed fine, but was told that she needed to be checked out by a doctor to make sure that she hadn't hurt herself too much.

Mrs Turnpike thanked the ambulance man as he left the three of them in the Accident and Emergency department.

'You'll be alright, poppet, they'll look after you now,' said the ambulance man as he waved to the lady on reception, and went back in the direction of the ambulance.

Mrs Turnpike chatted to the girls about school, and told them how excited she was about next term's topic, which was going to be aliens. Gemma really wished that she was in Mrs Turnpike's class, as she was so energetic and made everything seem so exciting. They began a long conversation about if aliens really existed or not. Mrs Turnpike was sure that they did; she said that she was really going to try hard to find some evidence of alien life. Gemma couldn't help but think that Mr Prince was all the evidence that they needed, but dared not say that to Mrs Turnpike. While they were chatting, Sal's mum arrived. She had bright purple hair, and wore a long flowing coat that looked like it was made out of carpet. She was rushing and looked very worried.

'Oh, Sal, what happened?' asked Sal's mum.

'I slipped and bumped my head. I feel quite alright now, Mum, but they said I have to see a doctor, to make sure I haven't hurt myself.'

'OK, sweetheart, don't worry,' replied Sal's mum kissing her on her forehead gently. 'Thank you for looking after her,' she said, looking at Mrs Turnpike. 'And thanks, Gemma, for staying with her - you're a good friend.'

'No problem at all. Will you be OK if Gemma and I head back to school now?' asked Mrs Turnpike.

'Oh yes, yes, thank you,' answered Sal's mum.

'Please let us know how she is when she's been checked over by the doctor, won't you?' requested Mrs Turnpike.

'Yes, of course, I'll call school and tell them what's what.'

Gemma hugged Sal and said she'd call her later. Mrs Turnpike touched Sal's hand and told her that she'd be OK.

On the way out of the hospital Gemma saw someone that she thought she recognised. As she got closer she realised that it was Santa, and she thought that he must be at the hospital visiting Mrs Santa.

'Hi, Santa,' sang Gemma as they approached one another.

'Oh hello, chicken,' replied Santa, who was obviously shocked to see her there. 'Everything OK, chick?' he asked. 'You haven't hurt yourself have you?'

'Oh no, I'm fine thank you, I came with my friend who bumped her head and knocked herself out,' replied Gemma with a smile. 'Are you here to see Mrs Santa?'

'Yes, chick, she's still not feeling well at all. They've asked me if I would like to stay here tonight. I really want to, but I'm worried about Seafa - she hasn't ever been left on her own overnight before.'

'Oh, Santa, I'll look after Seafa if that's any help. I can call in on my way home from school and check that she's OK. I know how to feed her, and I'd love to play with her,' gushed Gemma enthusiastically. Gemma liked Seafa much more than she liked Baldy, and she really wanted to help Santa out. He appeared very worried, and looked at least one hundred and eighty years old today.

'Would you do that for me, chicken?' asked Santa smiling. 'It really would put my mind at rest.'

'Of course I will,' said Gemma.

Santa gave Gemma details of where Seafa's food was kept, how much she needed to put in her bowl and the games she liked to play. He told her that Greg's mum had a key to his house, and said that he'd call her in a short while, to tell her about their arrangement. While all of this was going on, Mrs

Turnpike was once again on her mobile phone, being very efficient and organising teacher things.

*

Gemma and Mrs Turnpike left the hospital and walked towards the car park. She told Mrs Turnpike who Santa was, although she thought it best not to mention that she had recently stolen and returned his pants! As they walked, a car pulled up along side them, and Mrs Turnpike told Gemma to jump in the back and buckle up. Gemma was over the moon when she realised who the driver was. Apparently, Mrs Turnpike had called Mr Frazor to ask him to pick them up, and Gemma was thrilled to see him.

'Hello, Mr Frazor, are you feeling better now?' enquired Gemma thoughtfully.

'I'm much better now, thank you, how's the project coming along?'

'Ah, well, I haven't made any further progress because I still need your help. Please can I come and see you at lunchtime? I have the materials in my bag,' asked Gemma very excitedly.

'Sure you can, you know where to find me,' replied Mr Frazor, giving her the same nose-tapping signal that he had done some days ago.

Gemma smiled at Mr Frazor in the mirror, and eagerly looked through her bag to make sure that she had her pink wool. Mrs Turnpike and Mr Frazor chatted all the way back to school, while Gemma thought up games that she might play with Seafa.

Chapter 10

A Boring Prince

Gemma had only been back at school an hour when the lunchtime bell rang. However, an hour with Mr Prince sometimes felt like a fortnight. They had been studying World War II aircraft. Gemma had seen Mrs Turnpike's class running around the playground pretending to be aeroplanes. Through the flimsy classroom walls, she had also heard the exciting video that the other class were lucky enough to watch. Mr Prince had given each member of Gemma's class a plain piece of card with the name of an aircraft on it. Then, they had to go to the library and find a book about the aircraft and write about it. Gemma had suggested that they could get the tablets and do some internet research, but Mr Prince said that he had forgotten to plug the cabinet in, so the tablets weren't charged. Gemma did the best she could with the information that she could find. The exact aircraft that she was supposed to research wasn't in any of the library books, so she found a book with a plane in it, and asked Mr Prince if it would be OK if she used that one. Mr Prince looked at the book for less than three seconds and said 'mm.' It turned out that this particular aircraft wasn't used in World War II at all, but she'd completed almost a page of work now, so it was too late to do anything about it.

At last it was lunchtime, and Gemma was

determined not to let her opportunity get away. She went straight to the storeroom to find Mr Frazor, who was busily emptying out boxes of books onto the shelves.

'Hello, Mr Frazor, may I come in?' asked Gemma as politely as she could.

'Ahh, Gemma, pull up a chair and we'll get cracking.'

Mr Frazor spent the next forty minutes showing Gemma how to crochet. He had brought her some samples of things he had made, and he was very proud of his talent. Gemma listened carefully, and Mr Frazor was a patient and kind teacher.

'Why are you the caretaker and not a teacher?' asked Gemma.

'Well, when I was at school I didn't work very hard. I found some things really difficult and I wasn't very good at reading, so I stopped trying. I would have loved to be a teacher, but I didn't think I was clever enough. But, I went to college recently and passed my English exams and now I'm doing maths. There's one thing I've learned, Gemma, if we try hard enough, we can all be whatever we want to be; we can do whatever we want to do; it's never too late to start.'

'Will you be a teacher when you've passed your maths exam? I'd love to be in your class,' said Gemma encouragingly.

'No, I have to take lots more exams, but I'm determined to get there,' replied Mr Frazor.

Gemma was concentrating hard on learning how to crochet, and she was good at it. To look at her, you would have thought that she used her tongue to manoeuvre the wool, not a crochet hook. Every time she pulled the wool to the left, her tongue, which was dangling out of her mouth, would go to the left. When the wool was pulled to the right, her tongue would go to the right. Mr Frazor chuckled to himself as he watched her, and wished that he had been able to concentrate like Gemma could, when he was nine.

'Oops, excuse me,' said Gemma as her stomach did a loud and long growl.

'Haven't you eaten yet?' asked Mr Frazor.

'Not yet, I really wanted to learn how to do this before I had my lunch.'

'Do you know enough now to be able to do it yourself? Go to the dining hall now and you can always come back tomorrow. I'll help you again if you get stuck,' said Mr Frazor kindly.

'Please can I stay and do a little bit more, Mr Frazor? I'm really getting the hang of it and I don't need to do much more.'

'Well, you really do need to eat your lunch and I need to eat mine too. Let's eat lunch here now, and see how much time we have left, deal?' asked Mr Frazor.

'Deal,' replied Gemma, as a broad smile quickly spread across her face.

As it turned out, they only had a couple of minutes left after they had finished eating, so they agreed to meet again tomorrow.

Chapter 11

Seafa Cat and a Mad Dog

As promised, on the way home, Gemma went to Greg's house to get the key to feed Seafa. She took a moment to call her mum to let her know that she would be late home. Then, Greg's mum walked next door with her to Santa's house. As she opened the door, Seafa snuggled herself around Gemma's leg and purred. Gemma bent down to tickle her; Seafa was obviously lonely and was pleased to have someone to play with.

'Will you be OK to stay for about fifteen minutes?' asked Greg's mum.

'Yeah sure, that will give me plenty of time to feed Seafa and to play with her a little,' said Gemma.

'OK, I'll come back in fifteen minutes then.' Greg's mum was in the middle of cooking dinner, so she rushed off to make sure the potatoes weren't boiling dry.

Gemma chatted to Seafa while she got her cat food out of the cupboard, and put it into her bowl. While she filled up her water bowl, Seafa played in and out of her feet and meooowwwwwed and puuuuurrrrred sweetly. Gemma put the food and water on the floor; Seafa sniffed at it but didn't eat any. She tiptoed over to Gemma and looked up at her with her adorable green cat eyes and purrrrrrrred again. Gemma bent down and, immediately, Seafa jumped onto her lap and began to gently lick her hands. Gemma loved how soft and cuddly Seafa felt - she totally understood why Baldy was so in love with her. Gemma held and played with Seafa for the entire fifteen minutes, and Seafa continued to meoooowwwwww and purrrrrrr with gratitude. When it was time to leave, she kissed Seafa between her fluffy ears and told her that she would be back as soon as she could.

'Want a quick drink before you go home?' asked Greg's mum as she locked Santa's door and walked back to her own house.

'Oh yes please, I gave Seafa some water, but forgot to drink myself,' remarked Gemma.

'Come in then, love, is juice OK? Can you take one for Greg too, please?'

'Yes please, juice will be lovely.'

Gemma drank her juice straight down and wondered where Greg was. She looked through the garden window to see if he was outside but couldn't see him. However, she knew he wasn't too far away, because Baldy was now standing by her side wagging his tail.

'Do you know where Greg is, please?' asked Gemma.

'Oh yes, sorry, love, he's in the shed. Apparently he needs to make adjustments to the dog see-saw. That competition is taking over his entire life,' laughed Greg's mum.

Gemma walked up the garden to the shed, as did Baldy, who remained at her side.

'Hi, how's it going?' asked Gemma.

'Oh hi, I'm just trying to make this see-saw a bit less rickety. Hello, lad, I thought you were sleeping,' answered Greg, while he patted Baldy's head. 'Let's see if this is any better then, mate,' he said, as he made his way out of the shed and back to the see-saw section of the assault course. 'C'mon, Baldy.'

Gemma was holding onto the side of the shed, kicking the snow off her new wellies. As she did this, Greg quickly made a snowball and threw it at her back. He was always a good shot and simply couldn't resist messing about in the snow. Baldy was standing next to Gemma, watching everything she did. He jumped and shivered as the icy snowball shattered on Gemma's back, and then slid down to land on his head.

'Baldy, Baldy,' called Greg enthusiastically, but Baldy was too interested in Gemma to move. He shook the snow off his head, and stayed precisely where he was.

Gemma finished cleaning her new boots and walked to where Greg was fixing the see-saw.

'Good boy,' said Greg, noticing that Baldy had actually come over to where he was standing. 'OK, Baldy, try that, does it feel any better?' he asked, using his most encouraging voice. As predicted, Baldy didn't move or show any interest whatsoever in the see-saw. 'C'mon, Baldy, c'mon, up you come,' continued Greg. Still, Baldy did nothing. Gemma, noticing that Greg was a little down-hearted by Baldy's lack of interest and effort, thought it best if she left them to it; she really needed to be home soon anyway.

'I'd better get home, good luck with the training. I'll see you tomorrow.' Gemma walked into the house, leaving Greg in the garden to ponder his ideas about making the course more attractive for Baldy. She found Greg's mum and thanked her for helping her with Seafa and for the drink.

'Please can I call in on Seafa on my way to school tomorrow?' asked Gemma.

'Yes please, I'm sure Santa will be very grateful, he's never left her alone before. I'll pop in to see her later tonight as well - we'll keep her happy between us,' replied Greg's mum, smiling.

'See you in the morning,' called Gemma, as she began to walk out of the front door.

'Oh, hang on a minute, looks like Baldy wants to come to your house for tea,' chuckled Greg's mum. 'Baldy, Baldy,' she called. As usual, Baldy ignored her and remained right by Gemma's side.

'I think he must like my new boots,' said Gemma. 'He hasn't left my side since I arrived.' Greg's mum held onto Baldy's collar so that Gemma could leave the house without him. Baldy knew better than to growl at Greg's mum; he knew that she was in charge in this house, and wouldn't dare cross that line.

*

During the evening Gemma worked a little bit more on 0.3. She really wanted to finish it tonight so that she could show it to Mr Frazor tomorrow. However, she got into a bit of a tangle with the wool, so instead of showing him the finished product, she would be going back to ask for his help in fixing the mess.

Greg used his 'spoon of food' strategy to get Baldy round the course again, and the see-saw did appear to be more stable, so he was satisfied with that. He was still very concerned about how he was going to get Baldy over the competition course - he couldn't leave spoonfuls of food all over the place.

Chapter 12

Baldy Actually Moves

The following morning, Gemma got up earlier than usual to make enough time to go and see Seafa. She looked out of her bedroom window to see yesterday's snow still there, plus a little bit more that had fallen overnight.

After packing everything that she needed for the day, Gemma quickly sent Sal a text. She told her she would miss her at school today, and reminded her to enjoy watching daytime TV, and not doing schoolwork. Sal's mum had called last night to say that she had been allowed to leave hospital, but that she needed to rest for a couple of days, until her head didn't feel quite so sore.

By the time Gemma got to Greg's house, her wellies were very snowy so she slipped them off, and left them in the porch. Greg's dad came to the door and asked her to come in for a minute. He said that he didn't know where the key to Santa's house was, so she'd have to hang on for a little while. Greg was still upstairs brushing his teeth, but he shouted down a very frothy 'Morning Gem, I'll be down in a minute.' His mum was rushing around trying to find the key and Baldy was half asleep watching everyone from his basket.

'Morning, Baldy,' said Gemma, but today there

wasn't even a little flick of his tail to greet her, so Gemma left him to snooze.

'I popped in to see Seafa last night, she seemed happy enough, although she hadn't eaten her dinner,' said Greg's mum. 'Sometimes animals go on hunger strike as a protest when their owners are away,' she explained.

'Oh, I hope she's eaten it now,' replied Gemma in a concerned voice.

'Ah, a couple of missed meals won't hurt her. I expect Santa will be back later today anyway,' said Greg's mum, as she ushered Gemma out of the door waving the key to show her that she'd found it.

*

Seafa was sitting in the window as Gemma and Greg's mum walked up the path. When she saw them, she quickly jumped off the windowsill and sat behind the front door waiting for them to come into the house.

'Good morning, Seafa,' said Gemma, bending down to stroke her new friend. Seafa snuggled herself up to Gemma's knees and wriggled about, purring, as Gemma stroked her.

'Ahhh, you are a lovely little thing,' said Gemma. 'Let's see if you've eaten your dinner, shall we?' Before Gemma could stand up, Seafa jumped up into her arms and began licking her hands again. 'C'mon, snuggly, let's go into the kitchen,' said Gemma, still holding Seafa in her arms. Greg's mum was already in the kitchen; she was keen to know if Seafa had eaten or not.

'Her bowl's empty, love. You play with her for a minute and I'll fill her food and water up,' called Greg's mum from the kitchen. 'She's very pleased to see you.'

Gemma continued to snuggle, talk and play with Seafa. She thought that she might need some exercise so she ran up and down the hall, and Seafa followed her, meowing and snuggling around her feet whenever she could.

'All done, you ready?' shouted Greg's mum from the kitchen.

'Yes, I'm ready. Do you think they'd notice if I put Seafa in my pocket and took her to school with me today?' said Gemma jokingly.

'Mmm, I think you'd find it a bit tricky keeping her a secret,' replied Greg's mum, smiling.

'I'll call in again later, Seafa, I'm sure your daddy will be home soon,' said Gemma reassuringly.

'Meoooooowwwwwwwwww,' said Seafa, as if she understood every word that had been said.

'Oh, we're running late as usual, I hope Greg's got his coat on ready. You can come to school in the car with us this morning, we should just make it in time,' said Greg's mum.

'OK, that's great, thanks.' Gemma knew that she would keep nice and warm in the car, so this would avoid an embarrassing nose situation. She also knew that she could dodge T's Gang, and that was always something to be thankful for.

*

Greg was waiting in the hall with his coat on and his bag over his shoulder. He hated being late for school because his teachers always asked him why he was late, and he rarely knew what to say. His mum was always in a flap looking for this, or just doing that before they left the house, and Greg found that difficult to explain.

'Good boy, Greg, I just need to find my gloves and then we can go,' said Greg's mum, running around lifting things off chairs and searching her pockets.

'Oh, you're talking to me now, are you, Baldy?' asked Gemma, bending down to pat his head.

'Right, we're all set, wagons roll,' announced Greg's mum. Greg had absolutely no idea why his mum said this every morning. Whenever she said 'all set', he imagined himself as a red jelly man, wobbling down the path and into the car. And, whenever she said 'wagons roll', he imagined a wagon full of jelly people, including himself, driving down the road to school. What she was actually trying to communicate was, 'Get in the car, I've found everything I need.'

The children walked down the path to the car, chatting about what the day might bring.

'Baldy, Baldy,' shouted Greg's mum. '*You* can't go to school, come on, back in the house.' As usual, Baldy stayed where he was.

'Oh, do you want to come with us today, lad?' asked Greg, who was so pleased that Baldy had moved of his own accord that he was now patting and stroking him.

'Stop that, Greg, we'll be late! Baldy,' screeched Greg's mum again. Baldy didn't move an inch. Greg's mum ran down the path, grabbed Baldy by his collar and led him back into the house.

'What ever has got into that dog?' asked Greg's mum in a flustered voice.

'I think it's his training,' replied Greg. 'We're really starting to bond now. See ya later, Baldy,' he called, as his mum shunted the dog into the house and scurried back down the path towards the car.

'You know, Baldy doesn't always show it, but he loves me really,' said Greg happily.

'Yes, I'm sure he does,' replied Gemma. 'Not long to the competition now, just one more day. Are you nearly ready?'

'He can do it; he makes all of the jumps properly and he balances so well on the see-saw. It's just that I'm still having to put spoons of food out along the course to get him to move. I was really glad that he just followed me to the car - maybe he'll follow me around the course tonight.' Greg was very excited about Baldy's enthusiasm to follow him, and Gemma hoped that he was right.

Chapter 13

Toasty Smells and a Tricky Tangle

The morning at school passed slowly. In maths they were learning about fractions and Mr Prince had given the children three different worksheets to complete. Gemma quite liked the lesson as she got to do colouring and maths together. During the lesson there was a wonderful smell of hot buttered toast drifting its way around the school. It turned out that Mrs Turnpike had made children toast and asked them to cut it into half, quarters and eighths before they were allowed to eat it. As a special treat, she also made her class an extra slice of toast each to take out for breaktime. Gemma imagined what an eighth of a slice of toast must look like and decided that she would try to make one at home later. In English the children had to write about what it would have felt like hiding inside an Anderson shelter during an air raid. Mr Prince had pushed the boat out on this one, and had let the children watch a short video of a lady talking about her experience of this as a child. Of course, Mrs Turnpike had done this too, but she didn't stop there. After the children had watched the video, she covered their tables with dark cloths. Then she asked them to sit underneath their tables in the dark, while she played sounds of scary air raid sirens and bombs falling from the sky.

Then, she handed out torches and the children spent the rest of the lesson writing, in torchlight under their tables. Gemma wondered what she would have to do to get a transfer into Mrs Turnpike's class. However, she decided that this was probably impossible because if she transferred, everyone would want to transfer, and Mrs Turnpike's class would become too big.

*

The lunchtime bell rang and Gemma quickly made her way to the storeroom.

'Hello, Gemma, come in,' said Mr Frazor as she knocked and popped her head inside the room. 'How's it all coming along, then? Did you manage to do a little bit more yourself?'

'I had a go, but I'm sorry, I got into a bit of a tangle. Are you any good with woolly knots?' asked Gemma apologetically.

'Let's have a look, see if we can sort it out,' replied Mr Frazor kindly. Gemma handed him the bag with 0.3 inside. 'Hmm, it is in a bit of a pickle isn't it? I'm sure we can get it sorted, I think we just have to be patient and do a little bit of unpicking.'

Mr Frazor told Gemma that she could sit and eat her lunch with him, while he worked on unravelling the mess. Neither Gemma nor Mr Frazor noticed Mrs Dainty as she poked her head into the storeroom, to see who was chatting in there. When Gemma did finally realise, she wasn't really sure what to do. Mrs

Dainty glared at her with her eyebrows raised as if to say, 'What on earth do you think you're doing in here?'

With half a mouthful of sandwich, and keeping her eyes fixed on Mrs Dainty, Gemma gently nudged Mr Frazor's elbow. Mr Frazor didn't look up; he was right in the middle of a tricky tangle, so he just said 'Yes?' Gemma was too scared to chew now, so she tried nudging Mr Frazor again, hoping that this time he would look up and see their visitor. 'Hang on, I've almost got this bit sorted,' said Mr Frazor happily.

'Ha herrrrrrmmm,' coughed Mrs Dainty in order to get Mr Frazor's attention.

'Oh, hello, Delilah, oh, I do beg your pardon, I mean Mrs Dainty,'

'Hello, Mr Frazor,' said Mrs Dainty, smiling sweetly. 'Is Gemma helping you with something?'

'Erm, yes, yes she is,' replied Mr Frazor, smiling at Gemma in order to make her feel more comfortable. 'She's been helping me with my crocheting - you know it's a favourite hobby of mine,' he explained.

'Oh I see, that's very kind of you, Gemma,' said Mrs Dainty. 'Please make sure you both remember to eat your lunch,' she ordered, before her head disappeared from view.

'Pheeeeeeeeewwwwwwwww,' said Gemma when she was sure that Mrs Dainty had definitely left.

'Ahhhh, her bark is much worse than her bite you know,' commented Mr Frazor. 'She's lovely really! Shhhh, don't tell anyone.'

Gemma chuckled at Mr Frazor, and knowing that he could be trusted, said, 'I promise not to tell anyone that Delilah is lovely!' mimicking Mrs Dainty's bossy voice and mannerisms.

They smiled at one another, and by the end of lunchtime 0.3 was looking much neater. Gemma asked a couple of questions about how to avoid getting into the same tangle again, and said that she would have another go tonight.

*

The afternoon flew past. It was games, and Gemma loved games because it meant being out of the classroom. She always felt like games was an extended playtime, and wished that she could play hockey or netball during break times. However, there only ever seemed to be a football available, and the boys would grab this and make it a boys-only game, even though this was strictly against school rules. The sports coaches were loads of fun. One sports lesson the coach forgot to bring out the cones that make the goal posts, so he used children for cones instead! On another occasion it was a hot summer's day and the children had played an hour of rounders. They were all complaining of being too hot, so the coach got the hose pipe out and sprayed them all, including himself.

Today they played basketball indoors because of the snowy weather. The coach had stuck a picture of Mr Prince on the board at the back of one basket, and a picture of Mrs Turnpike on the other one. Mrs Turnpike's class aimed to hit Mr Prince's head, and

Mr Prince's class aimed to hit Mrs Turnpike's head. While this made all of the children laugh, Gemma thought that she might have played better if she was on the opposing team. She would have far rather thrown a ball at Mr Prince's head than Mrs Turnpike's. The score at the end of the match was 15-5. Apparently Mrs Turnpike's class were more than happy to whack Mr Prince on the head fifteen times.

Chapter 14

Ambuuuushhhhhhhhhhh!

Gemma and Greg met at the school gates to walk home. They stopped at the little shop at the bottom of Greg's road because Gemma wanted to see if the cat food was still on offer. Greg didn't have any money so he waited outside. Gemma didn't find any special offer cat food this time, but she did find T's Gang. In order to avoid them, she decided not to buy anything. Hoping that they hadn't seen her, she walked back down the special offer aisle, passed the chocolate and headed for the door.

'Hey, dopey,' called one of the gang. Gemma continued as if she hadn't heard him.

'Hey, you, dopey girl,' he called again. This time he'd walked over to Gemma and had his hand on her shoulder, so there was no ignoring him.

'Hi,' said Gemma, trying not to show any fear at all.

'You got any money, squirt?' said one of the other boys.

'Yes,' replied Gemma.

'Well, that's good then, give it here,' said the biggest of T's Gang.

'No,' answered Gemma in a very casual voice. 'Have you got any money? Will you give your money to me?' she asked. Once again T's Gang were shocked by Gemma's reactions. No-one had ever asked them for *their* money; no-one had ever dared. After the initial shock, one of the boys began to snigger. T, the biggest boy, shot him a glance which made him instantly quiet.

'OK, squirt, if you won't give it to us, we'll take it!' said T. 'Get her money lads,' commanded T.

'If you come any closer to me at all, I will scream so loudly that it will burst your ears,' warned Gemma, using her Mrs Dainty voice, that she had practised earlier in the day. Now her heart was beating far too quickly and she really, really wanted to run away.

'Cover her mouth, then get her money,' said T.

One of the boys stepped closer to Gemma so, as promised, she let out an almighty scream, 'AAAAAHHHHHHHHHHHHHHHHHHHHHHHHH HHHHHHHHHHHHHHHHHHHHHHHHHHHHHH HHHHHHHHHHHHHHHHHHHHHHHHHHHHHH HHHHHHHHHHHHHHHHHHHHHHHHHH.'
Gemma surprised herself with the volume and length of her scream. T's Gang covered their ears, a couple left the shop and the others backed away. The shop-keeper came dashing to find out what was going on, so Gemma stopped screaming.

'What were you making that dreadful noise for?' asked the tall, middle-aged shop-keeper.

'These boys were going to take my money and I couldn't think of any other way to protect myself,' answered a very out-of-breath Gemma.

'Oh, I see,' said the shop-keeper. 'We'll see about that!' She turned to face T and the other two members of the gang who remained in the shop.

'We didn't do anything, we don't even know her!' exclaimed T before he could be accused of anything.

'So, you didn't ask this girl for her money, is that what you're saying?'

'That's right. She's a nutter screaming like that!' sniggered T.

'OK, so, if I check the CCTV footage, I will see this young lady standing in my shop, alone, screaming will I?' asked the shop-keeper.

'Erm, erm, er...' said T, frantically looking around the shop to see where the cameras were, and where they were pointing.

'Exactly as I thought,' said the shop-keeper. 'I don't want you ever coming in here again, do you hear me? I won't have my customers scared by a group of little bullies - stay out of here and stay away from this girl! I could call the police and show them what's happened here. Do you want me to do that?'

'Erm, no, no don't do that, we'll leave her alone,' said T in a worried voice.

'Good, if I find out that you've done this again, you'll be in big trouble!' warned the shop-keeper as she wagged her finger at T. 'Go on, clear off!'

T, and the rest of the gang shuffled their way past Gemma, and out of the door.

Greg was hiding around the corner, waiting for Gemma to come out of the shop so that he could snowball her. Having already made the mistake of accidentally snowballing the couple who'd previously left the shop because of Gemma's noise, this time, when he heard the shop door-bell's ting, he was quite convinced that it had to be Gemma coming out. He hid around the corner for a second time, took aim, shouted 'AMBUUUUUUUSHHHHHHHHH,' and pelted the boys with the snowballs he'd made and stashed while he'd been waiting. The boys, already shaken by their experience in the shop, ran for their lives, not at all sure what was happening to them.

Realising his mistake, Greg remained hidden. So far he'd managed to miss his target twice, and was now all out of ammunition. He doubted that there was enough time to make more snowballs, but thought it worth a try nevertheless. Just as he bent down to begin to roll more snow, he heard someone running towards him. He turned to see Gemma, armed with a snowball running at him, full speed. She'd missed every shot she'd made in basketball today. It was difficult throwing at Mrs Turnpike because she liked her so much. However, she knew that Greg would have armfuls of snowballs ready for her; he always did. So, she decided to imagine that she was throwing at the picture of Mr Prince.

'YYYYYYAAAAAAAAAHHHHHHHHHH,' shouted Gemma as she lobbed the snowball in Greg's direction.

Greg quickly put his hand out to guard himself, but the snowball caught the edge of his glove and exploded just in front of his face. He had clumps of fluffy, white snow hanging off his hat, his eyebrows and his cheeks. Gemma was ecstatic about her shot. 'GOT YA,' she shouted as she quickly ran for cover, knowing that Greg would get her back twice as hard.

'I've got no ammo left; it's alright you can come out,' shouted Greg.

'Yeah yeah, I've heard that one before,' said Gemma, who'd been caught out with this trick previously.

'No, really I haven't. I used it all on the boys that came out of the shop before you - I thought it was you and pelted them,' shouted Greg laughing.

'NO WAYYYYYYYYYYY,' said Gemma in disbelief. 'Noooooooo wayyyy!'

Gemma popped her head round the corner, just to check that he was telling the truth. He was walking unarmed to where he knew she was hiding.

'No way what?' asked Greg.

'Greg, you just ambushed T's Gang. The boys that came out of the shop just before me, they were T's Gang. Did they know it was you? Did they see you?'

'Naaaaaah, I was hiding the whole time,' said Greg, very pleased with himself having ambushed the gang and got away with it. 'You were ages in the shop! I used some of my ammo on some other people that came out before them, I thought that was you too!'

'What?' asked Gemma.

'Yeah, someone came out of the shop, I thought it was you, so I snowballed them. Turned out not to be you, so I made some more ammo and waited. Then someone else came out, and I was sure it would be you, so I shouted "AMBUSHHHH" at them and used the rest of my stash. Straight after that, you came out and I'd got no snowballs left, so this is why I have a face full of snow!' said Greg, wiping his face on Gemma's shoulder.

'Wow, you got all of T's Gang. Both sets of boys

were part of the gang and you single-handedly ambushed them all,' laughed Gemma.

The children exchanged stories about what had happened inside and outside the shop. They concluded that between them they'd beaten T's Gang by mistake again.

As they approached Greg's house, Gemma commented that Santa must be back. When he asked her how she could possibly know, she said, 'Look, there are lots of footprints in the snow by his house.' Greg thought this was very clever, he didn't tell Gemma that he thought she was smart, but he made a mental note to use her technique whenever he could.

'Hi, kids, had a good day?' asked Greg's mum as they walked into the porch.

'Yes thanks, we've had some fun,' giggled Greg.

Gemma and Greg took off their boots and went into the kitchen for a drink before going to see Seafa.

'Hello, lad, you look nice and comfy in your basket,' said Greg, as he patted Baldy on the head and tickled his neck a little. Baldy wagged his tail to say hello.

'Now then, I've got a bit of bad news for you both,' said Greg's mum in a serious voice. 'Mrs Santa passed away last night. She's been ill for a long time, but it's still very sad news and of course Santa's terribly upset. He's very grateful to you, Gemma for looking after Seafa for him. He was able to stay at the hospital and be with her, well, you know when...' her voice trailed off. Neither Greg nor Gemma quite knew what to say or do. They could see that Greg's mum was close to tears, and wondered if they should cry too. Gemma had never met Mrs Santa, but she felt unhappy for Santa because he was a lovely man, and she worried that he might get lonely on his own.

'Is she still at the hospital, Mum?' asked Greg. He felt he had to say something, and this was something he wanted to know about so it made sense.

'Yes, love, she'll stay there until Santa's made arrangements with the funeral directors.'

'Will she come back home then?'

'Probably not; that used to happen years ago, but it rarely happens any more.'

Greg's gran had told him, that when her mum had died, she'd been brought home so that anyone that knew her could visit her to say their goodbyes. Greg had found this most odd, and the notion of bringing someone home to live with you for a few days after they'd died made him feel very uncomfortable. Greg let out a sigh of relief; he really didn't like the idea of Mrs Santa being next door and not being alive. Gemma was still very uncertain of what to say or do, so she sat with Greg and his mum and said, and did nothing.

'Oh, Gemma, Santa said he'd be really grateful of your help over the next few days. He's got lots of arrangements to make and he might have to be out of the house more than usual. He knows you love Seafa - would you mind still popping in to see her and making sure her food and water are full up?' asked Greg's mum.

'Yes, I'd love to. Do you think Seafa will be OK?

Will she know about Mrs Santa? Do animals get upset when people die?' she asked thoughtfully.

'You know, I think they probably do,' replied Greg's mum. 'But perhaps not quite in the same way as humans. She'll definitely need your hugs and tickles - she might be a little bit lonely I suppose.'

'What about Santa? Will *he* cry and will *he* be lonely, Mum?' asked Greg.

'Yes, I expect he'll get upset from time to time, and although he still has Seafa for company, he'll miss having Mrs Santa to chat to and share things with.'

Even though Gemma was worried that she wouldn't know what to say, or what to do if Santa cried, she decided it was better to go and see him, sooner rather than later.

'Is it OK if *we* pop next door now please?' asked Gemma. She'd stressed the 'we', in the hope that Greg's mum would know that she would rather all three of them went together today.

'I'm sure Santa will be really pleased to see you. He'll be able to tell you how you can help him over the next few days too,' replied Greg's mum.

*

Santa answered the door with his usual friendly smile. Greg's mum squeezed his hand, gave him a quick kiss on his cheek and told him that she'd brought him some apple crumble. She explained that she was baking anyway, so it was no trouble to make a portion for him. He thanked her and moved away from the door, so that they could all go into the house.

'Hello, lovely Seafa,' said Gemma, as the fluffy cat came to play around her feet. She bent down and picked Seafa up, who instantly snuggled into her arms and meowed as if to say hello back.

'Well, you two seem to be best buddies,' said Santa, smiling. 'You know, chick, she won't let me pick her up. She only lets Mrs Santa do that.' Everyone immediately realised what Santa had said, and no one quite knew what to say or do again.

'She looks very comfortable snuggling with you,' said Greg's mum, breaking the silence and trying to lift the mood a little.

Greg had heard people say that they're sorry when people had died, but he'd never quite understood why. He only usually said sorry if he'd done something wrong, so it didn't seem like the right thing to say just now. He wanted to play with Seafa for something to do, but Seafa only had eyes for Gemma.

'Shall I check on Seafa's food?' asked Greg

'Oh, yes please,' said Santa, Gemma knows where everything is, don't you, chick?'

Gemma smiled and made her way to the kitchen with Greg, with Seafa still curled up in her arms like a baby.

'Right then, where's her food kept?'

Greg sorted out Seafa's dinner and water bowl, while Gemma and Seafa continued to cuddle and play. Santa and Greg's mum were chatting quietly in the lounge.

'Do you think she'll come to me?' asked Greg.

'I don't know, I thought she was this friendly with everyone until Santa said he couldn't hold her. Do you want to try and take her and see if she'll go to you?'

'OK, let's try,' said Greg.

Gemma faced Greg and held Seafa out towards him. As Greg put his hands out, Seafa climbed up Gemma's arms and wrapped herself around her shoulder and nuzzled into her neck.

'Ah, she must really love my fluffy scarf,' said Gemma, gently stroking Seafa's furry tail that now curled just under her chin.

'Guess not then,' said Greg, a little disappointed. 'Maybe she only likes girls and not boys.'

'Well, I'm not sure about that, she's pretty keen on Baldy!' replied Gemma.

'You two ready?' called Greg's mum from the lounge.

'Yep, all sorted,' shouted Greg.

At the door, Greg's mum squeezed Santa's hand and gently kissed him again. Greg wondered if she'd always do this from now on; he didn't remember her doing it before, and wondered if his dad would mind.

'If you need anything, you know where I am,' said Greg's mum kindly.

'Thanks, and thank you for looking after Seafa,' replied Santa.

Gemma wanted to get home as early as she could because she wanted to continue with 0.3. She was quite sure that she could finish it tonight, if she didn't get the wool into a tangle again.

'Gem, I was searching on my computer and found a video clip of last year's dog training competition. Want to see it?' asked Greg excitedly.

'Oh OK, I can't stay long though, I have a project at home that I want to try to finish tonight,' explained Gemma.

Greg nattered on about how the course was reallllllllllly similar to the one he'd built in the garden for Baldy, and about how nervous he was becoming as the competition drew nearer. He told Gemma that the dogs were highly trained and that no one used spoons of food to get their dogs around the course.

Once inside the house, the children sat at the dining table to watch the clip. Greg continued to chatter on and on about how fantastic the dogs were and Gemma couldn't help but agree. They seemed to fly around the course effortlessly, looking like they were enjoying every moment of it. At the same time, Baldy seemed to effortlessly glide under the table and slide himself comfortably into Gemma's lap.

'Oh, hello, Baldy,' exclaimed Gemma, who was very surprised by his sudden show of affection.

'Where is he?' demanded Greg.

Gemma looked down onto her lap and stroked Baldy's head.

'He's here, on my lap!'

'What's going on, how come you've got animal magnetism all of a sudden? He's never climbed onto my lap! Sometimes he's climbed onto my bed, but he's never climbed onto me like that,' said Greg, shocked and disappointed.

'Baldy and I seem to be making friends, although he still ignores me whenever he wants to,' replied Gemma, trying to make Greg feel a little better. Baldy closed his eyes, and let out a long and comfortable sigh indicating how content and relaxed he was. They watched the end of the clip and had another look at the trophy.

'Wouldn't that trophy look great on my windowsill?' asked Greg, who was trying to remain positive even though he didn't think that Baldy stood a chance of winning it.

'Yeah, that would be ace,' replied Gemma, who was thinking exactly the same as Greg, but not saying it.

Gemma shuffled around and told Baldy that it was time for him to jump off, but he didn't want to move. She gave him a little push, but he was far too comfortable.

'Up you get, Baldy, it's time for me to go home,' said Gemma, slowly standing up. Baldy unwillingly slid off her lap, stood at her feet and looked longingly up at her. 'Good boy,' she said, patting him gently on his head. 'Gotta get home, I want to finish something tonight.'

Gemma grabbed her coat and shouted bye to Greg's mum. She went into the porch to put her wellies on and noticed that Baldy was at her side again.

'See you tomorrow,' said Gemma.

'OK, c'mon, Baldy, what's it with you and Gemma?' Greg was now clearly very irritated by Baldy's fascination with Gemma. He held onto his collar, even though he was growling, while Gemma quickly stepped out of the door.

Chapter 15

Ping, Plop, Thud

Having spent every spare moment that evening very carefully crocheting 0.3, it looked exactly as Gemma had imagined it, and now she needed to decide how to keep 0.3 attached to her nose. She had two ideas for this. One, was to thread elastic all around the edge of the circle. She thought that this would pull the edges in, and 0.3 would grip onto her nose. A little bit like how the elastic on the top of your socks grips your leg. Her second idea was to use 0.3 like a pirate's eye patch. The only difference being that it would cover her nose instead of her eye!

Being a logical girl, Gemma decided to try her first idea first. She got some elastic, and measured it around her nose. It was difficult to estimate how tight it would need to be pulled to keep 0.3 on her nose, so, she chose to cut the elastic longer than she thought she needed, thread it through, and try. It only took about half an hour to complete. Gemma popped 0.3 on her nose, and went to the bathroom mirror to see how it looked. It felt just a little bit too tight, but was quite bearable and there were no dangly, tickly bits this time. She was very pleased with how 0.3 looked. She turned to her left and right to examine from all angles. A huge smile spread over her face, as she realised she had finally created the perfect nose warmer.

However, as she smiled, her nose wrinkled up a little and PIIIIIIIIIIIIIINNNNNNNNGGGGGG. Off popped 0.3! The small, pink, woolly warmer, went flying through the air. Gemma put her hands out to try to catch it but there was no chance. 0.3 was travelling too fast, and before she could blink, her beautiful pink nose warmer had landed *plop*, into the toilet. She looked down in horror, and watched as the toilet water began to seep into 0.3.

'Noooooooooooo,' shouted Gemma as she frantically tried to think of what to do. Should she use her hand to fish 0.3 out immediately, before it took on so much water that it sank to the bottom of the toilet bowl? Should she get something to poke it out with? Gemma quickly looked around the room to see what she could use. Toothbrush! Ewwwww, no, no, no. Toilet cleaning brush! Ewww, again no. Gemma imagined what the toilet brush had previously scrubbed off the toilet, and didn't want 0.3 coming into contact with that. Hair brush! Noooo, she'd never be able to brush her hair with it ever again, knowing it had been down the loo!

It was no good. She took a deep breath and bravely put her hand inside the toilet. She slowly dipped her finger-tips just under the water and grabbed 0.3. As she lifted it out of the water, she realised she had no idea what she was going to do with it now that it had been retrieved. She dangled 0.3 over the toilet as the smelly water, drip, drip, dripped out of it. In one very swift movement, Gemma flung 0.3 into the sink and turned on the tap. At that moment, 0.3 seemed to jump into life. As the water hit it, it slid down into the plug hole and wriggled about. Gemma thought 0.3 looked like a small pink mouse trying to escape from being drowned. She didn't know whether to continue to drown the mouse, so that it was clean and usable again, or save it from the torture of the cold water tap! Instead of saving the poor creature, Gemma grabbed some shower gel and squirted it at it. It's response was to froth and bubble. Seeing as she had got this far, Gemma decided to go the whole way. She began scrubbing and smacking 0.3 to make sure that there would be no trace of toilet left whatsoever. She couldn't help wonder what noise a little pink mouse might make if it were to receive this treatment, so she stopped. Now, I know you've had trouble with this before, remember the puppy-dog ears? Come on, clear your mind of poor little pink mice being half drowned and beaten to death. I'm sure they wouldn't be as noisy as you're imagining! Squealy squeaks are not very pleasant to think about so, STOP IT!

When Gemma was quite sure that 0.3 was toilet-free, she carefully squeezed the remaining water out and wondered where best to dry it. 0.3 was quite small so she needed to make sure that wherever she put it, it wouldn't get lost. Eventually she decided on putting it on the radiator in her bedroom so that, when it was dry, she could try to make adjustments to correct the 'piiiiiiiinnnnnnnnngggggggg' factor.

*

Meanwhile at Greg's house, Baldy had been put through his paces and had had his dinner while training. He was now very good at balancing on the see-saw, and made all of the jumps really easily. Greg tried to get Baldy to sit on his lap, while he watched the video clip of last year's show again. But Baldy had worked hard for his dinner and looked like he was settled into his basket for the rest of the night. Greg took his laptop over to Baldy, got down on the floor and had a good chat to him.

'Look at that lovely trophy, Baldy!' said Greg, patting and stroking his friend. 'We can win that, I know we can. You're a very clever dog and really good at the assault course now.' Baldy wagged his tail and let out a contented sigh. Greg played the video to him, whilst giving a running commentary about what the dogs were doing. He pointed out that the dogs got a treat *after* they had finished the course, and not all the way through. He really hoped that Baldy would get the hang of that soon.

'Only one more training session left, lad. The competition's the day after tomorrow, not long now!' said Greg, using his most encouraging voice. Baldy shuffled around a little, as if to say, 'Are we done yet?' As Baldy shuffled, Greg noticed that there was a piece of material hanging over the side of his basket, and stretched over to see what it was.

'What's that doing in there, mate? I bet Gemma's been looking for that!' Greg carefully pulled on the end of the material, to reveal Gemma's scarf. Baldy wriggled about as the scarf was pulled from under his tummy. 'She must have dropped it in there earlier,' mumbled Greg, as he walked into the hall to hang the scarf up for Gemma to collect tomorrow.

'AARRRRRRGGGGGGGGHHHHHHHHHHHHH HHHH,' shouted Greg, falling backwards, landing with a thud on the floor. 'Ahhh, ohhhh, my, ohh that hurt,' he moaned.

'Hooooooo,' moaned Baldy, 'hoooooooooooooooooooooo.'

'Oh, lad, I'm so sorry, how did you get there?' asked Greg, while he quickly moved his legs off his little squashed dog. Baldy stood up and shook himself off. 'Are you alright, Baldy, did I hurt you?' Baldy stared up at Greg, wagged his tail and appeared unharmed. Greg ruffled his ears and tickled him under his chin, 'Aahhhhh, lovely dog,' he said. And then it dawned on him.

'YEEEEEEEESSSSSSSSSSSSSSSSSS,' shouted Greg, 'YEEEEEEEEEESSSSSSSSSSSSSSSSSSSSSS,' you've got it, Baldy. The reason Greg had never fallen over Baldy before, or indeed even worried that he might, was because Baldy had never followed him before! Greg was very excited about this. He hugged and patted Baldy and told him how fantastic he was. If Baldy had followed him into the hall, then there was a chance that he might follow him around the assault course. Filled with hope, Greg went back to Baldy's basket, picked up his laptop and watched last year's video clip again. He called for Baldy to join him, as he was quite sure that watching the video had helped him to become a more obedient dog. However, Baldy had curled himself up on the hall floor and was already snoozing happily. 'OK, lad, you've done enough work for today, you enjoy your snooze,' said Greg kindly.

Chapter 16

Concentrate on the Good Stuff :)

Gemma had checked 0.3 every half an hour, but by bed time it was still wet. She checked again the following morning and now it was completely dry. Even though she didn't have time to make the adjustments that she had planned, she decided to wear 0.3 on her walk to feed Seafa before school anyway. Seeing as she walked most of the way alone, she reckoned that she wouldn't be doing that much smiling, so 0.3 should be reasonably safe. She was very excited about trying it out, and knew that Mr Frazor would be proud of her for finishing it herself.

Gemma looked in the hall mirror before she left the house. 0.3 was hardly visible really, it looked much better than the previous versions and so far, seemed a lot more practical too. However, this could not be said for the scarf she was wearing today. As she had misplaced her usual scarf, she was wearing her old one, that she used to wear when she was in Year 1. It had pictures of penguins and polar bears on it. Gemma didn't like wearing it now for many reasons:

1. It was too small, and only just fitted around her neck.
2. She'd worn that scarf when she had been to an ice-skating birthday party. That was

actually the only time she had ever been ice skating. All she could remember about the event, was that she spent most of the skating time on the floor, waiting for someone, anyone, to help her to stand up. This was then followed by a birthday party which consisted of two hours of dithering in soaking, icy, wet jeans with everyone planning their own birthday parties at the same venue! Followed by a week of blistered feet from the dreadful, blue, hired skates. People do that for fun?

3. She'd seen several boys wearing this scarf, and wasn't sure if it was actually meant to be for girls at all.

4. On one foggy morning, Gemma's mum had made her wear this scarf for school. As usual, it was a lovely sunny afternoon so she'd stuffed the scarf into her bag. When she got home, she realised that one of her pens had leaked into her bag. Now, the biggest penguin, the one right at the front, looked like he had an inky black eye.

5. It was itchy. She was always desperately uncomfortable when she wore it, but would be terribly cold today if she didn't wear it.

6. It had stupid little pompoms dangling from strings on it. When she was little, the pompoms used to trip her up all the time, and she still had a scar on her knee from one such incident.

Nevertheless, she didn't have any choice today. It was stupid, ridiculously small, pompom, penguin, scarf, or nothing. She did her best to cover it up with her coat and set off to go and check on Seafa.

*

Greg was in a particularly good mood when Gemma arrived to get the key for next door. He gave her a lovely broad smile as he opened the door to let her in, and immediately rattled on and on about how Baldy had followed him.

'Oh, that's fantastic progress, will he follow you anywhere now?' asked Gemma, hoping that Baldy had finally decided to help Greg out a little.

'Not exactly, but if he's done it once, I know he can do it again,' said Greg. Gemma couldn't help but think that Greg had to be the most optimistic person she'd ever known. He always concentrated on the positive things, and was rarely put off when things didn't go exactly as he planned. He was always willing to keep going, even when things seemed impossible.

'Argh.' said Gemma, struggling to loosen her itchy, uncomfortable scarf, whilst making her way to the kitchen to say hello to Greg's mum. She had already removed 0.3, after the seventh piiiiiiinnnnnnnggggggg, which occurred only moments after she had left her house. Apparently, any facial movement at all caused 0.3 to run for its life! She licked her lips, piiiiiing. She moved her chin, piiiiing. She raised her eyebrows, piiiiiing. Gemma hadn't realised how regularly she moved parts of her face: sniff, piiiiiing, yawn, piiiiiing, shiver, piiiiiiing, the list went on and on. Taking Greg's optimism and perseverance as inspiration, she planned to show 0.3 to Mr Frazor at lunchtime, and then continue to work on it until it was perfect.

'Morning,' chirped Gemma.

'Morning, love, I'll just grab the key and we'll pop next door,' replied Greg's mum.

Gemma noticed that Baldy's basket was empty, and she was instantly worried that he might have left home again. However, she soon realised that there was absolutely no need to worry as she saw both Greg and Baldy walking together up the hall, towards the kitchen.

'Here you are, you left this here yesterday,' said Greg, handing Gemma her scarf.

'Oh double wow,' said Gemma, as she pointed to just behind Greg. Baldy had followed him from the front door to the kitchen, and Greg was elated.

'What a fantastic dog you are,' shouted Greg, while he patted and tickled Baldy's face. 'You see, I told you he could do it! Good boy, Baldy, good boy.' Greg's excitement made everyone smile, and Gemma was doubly happy with the return of her scarf.

'Come on then, let's get next door, we don't want to be late for school,' said Greg's mum.

'OK, I'm ready,' replied Gemma, hoping that she would have enough time to swap her scarf when she got back from feeding Seafa.

At Santa's house, the mood was entirely different. He answered the door with his usual smile, but it was easy to see that deep inside he was very sad.

'Morning, chicken, thanks for popping in. I think Seafa really needs your cuddles today; she feels a little bit lost, like I do, I reckon,' said Santa with a faint smile.

Greg's mum gave Santa a friendly hug, and they went off into the lounge to chat as usual. Seafa was already at Gemma's feet, so she picked her up, chatted to her and cuddled her as she got her food and water sorted out. Even though she hated her stupid, pompom, penguin scarf, it appeared that there was some good in it after all. Seafa loved it! She batted the pompoms with her fluffy little paws, and watched them flick around Gemma's shoulders.

'Oh, you're such a lovely, lovely, little kitty,' said Gemma, stroking and kissing Seafa as she played.

Chapter 17

Fab Friday

'Hellllllloooooooooo', shouted Gemma as she arrived in the playground to find Sal waiting for her. 'How's your lumpy head?'

'It's fine, thanks,' replied Sal with a smile. 'Have I missed much? Oh, thanks for your texts by the way.'

'You're welcome, and no, you've missed nothing. Mr Prince is our teacher, remember?' replied Gemma sarcastically.

The girls chatted about their ride in the ambulance, and about how lovely Mrs Turnpike had been. As they walked towards their classroom, Sal's carrier bag began to split and the contents started to empty themselves out. She was leaving a trail of stuff behind her, including a small toy car, an empty pencil case, the pens and pencils that should have been in the pencil case, and her lunch. She was always in a pickle with her things, and Gemma was forever helping her to find stuff she'd lost, and picking up things she'd dropped. As they didn't have another carrier bag, they decided to put everything into Gemma's bag, and find a new carrier bag when they were inside the classroom. However, as they approached their classroom they both realised that today was not an ordinary day. The tables in Mrs Turnpike's class had been arranged so that children were no longer sitting together. Mr Prince was sitting at his desk while a few of the children began to do the same in his classroom, and poor Sal was filled with terror.

Today was Fab Friday. Fab Friday, had been invented by Mrs Dainty because, Testing Tuesday, had not gone down too well with the parents, teachers or children. Fab Friday, happened on the last Friday of each month. Every child from Year 1 upwards, spent the whole morning doing maths, English and science tests. Then the following Friday, the children who had made the most progress since the last, Fab Friday, got to go onto the stage during assembly, shake hands with Mrs Dainty, and receive a sticker and a lollipop. Gemma had been on the stage a couple of times, and found the going-on-the-stage thing, much more difficult than the tests. The testing didn't really bother Gemma at all; whether they called it Testing Tuesday, or Fab Friday, she always tried her hardest and generally got good results. However, Sal was always completely terrified by it. She had initially renamed, Testing Tuesday, to Totally Terrible Tuesday, because that's how she felt about it. Then, when it was renamed to, Fab Friday, she still felt no better and, renamed that to, Frightening Friday.

Today, Sal looked into the classroom and was rooted to the spot. Gemma tried to distract her by getting a carrier bag and asking her to help fill it up with her stuff, but poor Sal was completely terrified. Mr Prince called the children into the room, took the register and began the tests. Gemma had tried to tell Mr Prince that Sal wasn't feeling too comfortable, but he'd simply said 'mm' and handed out the test papers. However, in complete contrast to this, the children in Mrs Turnpike's class loved Fab Friday. Lots of them always went on stage and told wonderful recounts of their lessons.

As Gemma's lessons were about as exciting as the testing, she had been lost for words when she went on stage to receive her sticker and lollipop. She'd said something like, 'Erm, I learned about division using a computer game at home.' Some of the teachers sitting around the edges of the room visibly winced at what Gemma said, but Mr Prince didn't even bat an eyelid; as usual, he wasn't listening.

At the end of the tests, Mr Prince asked the children to read in silence, until the bell went for lunchtime. In contrast, Mrs Turnpike's class were having a celebratory dance around the room to one of the biggest pop hits of the year. Sal, like Gemma, would usually complain about how she wanted to be in Mrs Turnpike's class, but right now, she was so relieved that the tests were over, she didn't care what they were up to next door. Gemma, on the other hand, imagined them dancing and eating chocolate cake, while Mrs Turnpike joined in and told them all how marvellously they'd done. Gemma decided that it was no good dwelling on the negatives; she was going to be more like Greg and concentrate on all the good things. When the bell went for lunchtime, she told Sal she'd meet her later and skipped off to see Mr

Frazor, happy that she thought she'd done well in the tests.

*

Gemma tapped on the door of the storeroom, and popped her head around to look inside. Usually, Mr Frazor was sitting at his table, fiddling with a piece of school equipment that needed fixing. However, today, he had his head down on his table and was snoring softly. Gemma had no idea what to do. Should she leave him to sleep or wake him up? Would Mrs Dainty be cross if she caught him sleeping at work? Would Mr Frazor be cross if Gemma woke him up? All these thoughts were flying around her head, just as Mrs Dainty appeared behind her.

'Oh, hello, Gemma, are you here to help Mr Frazor again?' enquired Mrs Dainty in her haughty voice.

'YES, I'M HERE TO HELP MR FRAZOR,' shouted Gemma whilst also bashing the bottom of the door with her shoe, in the hope that Mr Frazor would be woken by the noise.

'Well, let's see if he's in here then, shall we?' said Mrs Dainty, forcing her not so dainty way past Gemma and into the storeroom. Mr Frazor remained how Gemma had found him, snoring gently, oblivious to the world. 'Ahh, he's right here, look,' said Mrs Dainty affectionately. She put the back of her hand against his face and gently brushed his cheek. 'Wakey wakey, Brian, oh, erm, Mr Frazor,' cooed Mrs Dainty softly.

Mr Frazor kept his eyes closed, breathed in deeply,

stretched his arms up into the air and said, 'Ahhhh, that feels so much better.' Then, as he opened his eyes, he flashed a lovely wide grin at Mrs Dainty, who flashed an equally wide grin back at him.

'Gemma's come to help you,' said Mrs Dainty, moving to one side so that Gemma could more easily be seen. Gemma gave a little wave, and Mr Frazor tapped the chair next to his, motioning her to come and sit next to him.

'Well, I'll leave you two to it; I expect you have lots to get on with. Please remember to eat your lunch,' reminded Mrs Dainty. 'Both of you,' she said, looking over the top of her glasses, and leaving the room.

'See, I told you she was lovely,' said Mr Frazor, smiling happily. 'So, how is your crocheting coming along?'

Gemma reached into her pocket and proudly presented 0.3.

'Oh wow, you've finished it... I think,' said Mr Frazor, while wildly racking his brain to try to think of a use for such an item.

'I concentrated really hard on not getting the wool into a muddle last night. I'm really pleased that I can crochet now, thanks Mr Frazor,' said Gemma.

'Wonderful, once you know how to do the stitches, you can make whatever you like,' replied Mr Frazor. 'Erm, now that we've got this far, would it be impolite of me to ask what it is that you're actually making?'

'Oh, I forgot that you didn't know,' replied Gemma, popping 0.3 onto her nose. 'It's a nose warmer!' she exclaimed. She could see that he loved her idea. His smile was wider than ever and she couldn't help but smile back. However, this time she was ready. As 0.3 pinged energetically off her nose, she swiftly put her hands out and caught it, like a championship goal keeper.

'What a catch,' laughed Mr Frazor. 'I'm guessing that that's not the first time that's happened then?'

'No, it pings off every time I move my face. I won't tell you where it landed the first time it pinged off - it's better you don't know about that!' replied Gemma.

'Hmm, let's see what we can do about keeping it on your nose then,' said Mr Frazor, holding onto his chin and staring into the distance.

'I had an idea about attaching elastic to it like a pirate's patch. Do you think it would work?' asked Gemma.

'Ah, what a super idea! I've got some elastic somewhere in here; let me hunt it down and we'll give it a go. You start your lunch so that we don't get into trouble with the boss, OK?'

'Yep, OK,' said Gemma, feeling very excited that 0.3 might soon become 0.3.1, with a little help from Mr Frazor. Gemma absent-mindedly opened the tin foil around her sandwiches and took a bite, while she daydreamed about what 0.3 would look like with extra elastic. Within seconds, she was racing around the storeroom saying 'Mmm mm, mmm mm,' desperately trying to find a bin.

'What's up?' asked a very concerned Mr Frazor.

'Bnnn,' said Gemma, trying hard to keep the food that she so desperately wanted to get *out* of her mouth, *in* her mouth.

'You need a bin?' enquired Mr Frazor, realising that she was in a hurry.

'Mmm, mm,' replied Gemma, nodding her head frantically. Mr Frazor ran to the bin by the door and quickly handed it to her. She put her head as far into the bin as it would go, and violently spat the mouthful of sandwich out, making sure that every tiny crumb was in the bin.

'Oh dear, oh dear, are you feeling unwell?' asked Mr Frazor, who was most concerned that she might throw up in his storeroom.

'I'm perfectly fine now, thank you,' she replied as she examined her sandwiches. 'I think I've got Sal's lunch and she's got mine. She had a bag catastrophe this morning and we put all of her things into my bag. I'm pretty sure that my mum didn't make me a banana, mushroom and brown sauce sandwich!'

'Surely, no one would make a banana, mushroom and brown sauce sandwich?' replied Mr Frazor, who was now also examining what was lurking in between the two perfectly innocent-looking pieces of bread.

'Oh what's that?' he asked, having never seen anything like it in a sandwich before in his life. He got his pen and started to gently poke at the mystery ingredient, turning it over while trying to fathom what it could be.

'I think it's a baked bean,' said Gemma, who was not at all sure that she was right.

'Oh yes, I think it might be,' replied Mr Frazor, who

was relieved that it was actually something edible.

'Please may I go and swap my sandwiches with Sal? I don't want Mrs Dainty to be cross with me, and I definitely can't eat these!' remarked Gemma.

'Course you can, I'll get the elastic while you're gone, and I'd better eat my sarnies too; I don't want to be in trouble either!'

*

Within a couple of minutes, Gemma was back in the storeroom. Apparently Sal was very grateful for the return of her lunch. Banana, mushroom, brown sauce and baked bean sandwiches were her favourite. She'd turned her nose up at Gemma's ham and tomato sandwiches, saying that they were tasteless and not very filling. Gemma ate while Mr Frazor got some scissors to cut a length of elastic. They chatted, ate, and worked through lunch until finally 0.3.1 was finished. Gemma tried it on and Mr Frazor made her laugh to see if it would ping off. Nothing! He raised his eyebrows and Gemma copied; still nothing. They put their tongues out, still nothing. It appeared that 0.3.1 was a success! Gemma said that she'd wear it for a while and report back to Mr Frazor to tell him how she'd got on.

'I could make one for you, if it turns out that it works OK,' said Gemma generously. Mr Frazor wasn't really sure what to say. He was pleased that he'd helped Gemma with her creation, but not sure if he wanted one himself.

'Erm, OK, you let me know if it works,' said Mr Frazor, realising that the most absurd things seemed to catch on. *I mean, whoever would have thought that teenage boys and girls would rush out to buy onesies thinking that they were cool - even though this is exactly what their parents dressed them in the day they were born. The only difference is that for babies it's called a sleepsuit!*

*

So, 0.3.1 was on its maiden voyage. Greg hadn't really asked much about Gemma's project, and Gemma, being sensitive about her nose, didn't usually volunteer information.

'Erm, what's that for?' asked Greg as they walked home from school.

'It's called 0.3.1 and it's my very own creation,' said Gemma proudly.

'Hmm, OK. But, what does it do?' asked Greg.

'It's a nose warmer,' she replied, as if he should have already known. Because she hated her nose being red, she automatically thought that everyone else did too.

'I see,' said Greg, who had nothing else to offer on that subject, but plenty when it came to talking about the dog competition. He talked pretty much non-stop all the way home, going on and on about how good the trophy would look on his windowsill. Gemma didn't like to spoil his dream, but still thought that there was absolutely no chance that

Baldy would win. However, she said nothing and reminded herself to be more like Greg. She told herself to concentrate on the positives, and do what you can to solve the negatives.

When they arrived at Greg's house, his mum looked at Gemma, tilted her head to one side, but chose not to ask about 0.3.1. She thought that Gemma had a plaster on her nose, like she had bumped it or something. As usual she made the children drinks and got the key ready to visit Santa. Baldy wagged his tail when he saw Greg, and Greg fussed and patted him to say hello.

'I'm going to get the course ready in a minute, lad –

let's see if you can do it without the food today. I promise to give you an extra-big dinner if you do the course first. Do we have a deal, dog?' Greg then picked Baldy's paw up, and shook it while saying, 'Deal human, let's go get that trophy,' in his best dog voice. Gemma and Greg's mum both laughed at Greg pretending that Baldy could talk. 'C'mon, lad, let's get cracking,' encouraged Greg as he tried to lure Baldy to the back door, waving his empty dinner dish in front of his nose. Baldy didn't budge.

'Oh, it seems that Baldy is a scarf thief,' said Gemma, noticing that her stupid, pompom, penguin scarf was sitting in the back of his basket.

'What, again?' exclaimed Greg, looking back to see the scarf scrunched up in the corner of the basket. 'That's weird, I've never known him do that before, I'm really sorry.'

'Oh, it's not a problem, Baldy can keep that one if he likes - it makes me itch and it's too small now. He's got the same taste as his girlfriend; Seafa loved playing with the pompoms this morning.'

Greg picked up the scarf and hung it on the back door, next to Baldy's lead. Baldy trotted over to where Greg was and watched everything that he was doing.

'Oh my goodness, it seems you're a very good dog trainer,' said Greg's mum in amazement as she watched Baldy follow Greg to the door.

'Fantastic, Baldy,' shouted Greg, 'you're a superb little dog.'

They finished their drinks and went to look after Seafa with Greg's mum. Santa was pleased to see them as usual, but Gemma still sensed his sadness. Seafa was really used to Gemma feeding her now, and instantly jumped into her arms when she bent down to stroke her.

'Oh, I don't have the pompoms for you to play with, sorry, Seafa. It seems Baldy likes them too. Maybe you two could share them next time you go out on a date,' said Gemma, smiling to herself. The fluffy kitty snuggled into her neck and purred while she tickled her tummy and kissed her nose. Gemma sorted out the food and water, and washed her plastic mat that sat under her bowl.

'Ready?' called Greg's mum from the lounge.

'Yes, I've finished,' replied Gemma, wishing that she could spend just a little while longer with Seafa.

'Would you mind opening the back door please? Seafa needs a bit of fresh air. She hasn't really been out today, and the cat flap is locked,' called Santa from the lounge.

'Yep, no problem,' replied Gemma, opening the door and carrying Seafa into the garden.

As she stepped outside, Gemma could hear Greg over the fence. He was calling Baldy to come outside. She put Seafa down on the snowy grass, and told her to have a little run around. Seafa, jumped up off the grass and onto the fence. Then, she cleverly tiptoed all the way along the fence until she was at the top of the garden. Greg saw her, and did his very best to pretend that she wasn't there. However, Baldy instantly ran to the top of the garden. He stood directly underneath Seafa, and she carefully jumped down off the fence to land at his side.

'Noooooo,' shouted Greg. 'It's our last training session! Please, Seafa, go back home, Baldy has work to do.' Seafa and Baldy ran around together, completely ignoring Greg, who thought that he must be inaudible. However, Gemma had heard him quite clearly, and felt awful that she hadn't thought about Seafa distracting Baldy during his last session. If she had given it a little thought, she would have asked Santa to let Seafa out a bit later. She was very cross with herself, but knew there was no point calling Seafa to come back if she was with Baldy.

Gemma and Greg's mum arrived back, to find Greg sitting in the kitchen with his head in his hands.

'I'm so sorry, I didn't think about Baldy's training. Santa asked me to let Seafa out for some air, and I just didn't think,' said Gemma apologetically.

'Don't worry, we'll have to enter the competition as we are. I guess one day won't really make a difference. I just wanted to see if he would follow me around better today, you know, without the food.'

'I know, I'm sure he will when he's less distracted. Sorry, Greg,' repeated Gemma. After making arrangements about where to meet at the competition tomorrow, Gemma said her goodbyes. She asked Greg's mum if she would check on Seafa over the weekend, just in case Santa was too busy and forgot to feed her.

*

Gemma was miserable as she walked home. She didn't like letting her friend down and wondered if there was anything that she could do to make things better. Today, she'd had both success, with 0.3.1, and failure with letting Seafa distract Baldy. Trying to take a leaf out of Greg's book, she decided to think of only the good things that had happened and made a list of them in her head.

1. 0.3.1 was firmly fixed to her nose and had stopped it getting red on the way to Greg's house.
2. Fab Friday tests had gone well, and she didn't have to dread the results.
3. Baldy had started to follow Greg sometimes.
4. She'd finally got rid of her stupid, penguin, pompom scarf.
5. Sal was back at school and her head was better. Even though she'd thought that it might explode doing the tests, she'd managed and was fine.
6. It was Friday! No school tomorrow, and, she could look forward to a day out with Greg at the competition.

Gemma ran through the list one more time, to make sure that she hadn't forgotten anything. She thought about all the things that had been good or made her smile during the day. Sal, Mr Frazor, Greg, Baldy, Seafa. But, Seafa wasn't on the list! She thought about Seafa playing with the pompoms on her scarf and it made her smile again. She thought how both Baldy and Seafa had enjoyed something that she didn't like at all. Drifting off into Gemma dreamland, she wondered what it was about the scarf that the animals liked. Seafa clearly liked the pompoms, but why did Baldy like it?

Chapter 18

Aaahhhhhhhaaaaaaaaa

Gemma sat bolt upright in bed. She'd been trying to figure something out all afternoon, but it wasn't until she put her brain to bed that it finally hit her. Baldy didn't really like the stupid, pompom, penguin scarf! What he really liked was Seafa. He was attracted to the scarf because Seafa had played with it, and he must be able to smell her on it. She began to piece various bits of information together. Baldy had been transfixed by the tumble dryer that contained Seafa's blanket; everyone had thought he was hypnotised by the machine going round and round. If this midnight brainwave was correct, it wasn't the machine he was interested in, it was Seafa's blanket inside. It must have smelled like Seafa.

She thought about the times that Baldy had followed her and realised that he only ever did this, after she'd been playing with Seafa. He'd sniffed around her new wellie boots, but only after Seafa had snuggled herself around them. He'd put her best scarf in his basket, but only after Seafa had curled herself around Gemma's neck. He'd sat on Gemma's lap at the table, but only after Seafa had sat on her lap first. So, why had Baldy followed Greg? Seafa wouldn't go anywhere near him when he'd tried to hold her, so he definitely didn't smell like Seafa.

Gemma tried to remember when, exactly, Baldy had been obedient and stood by Greg. The first time, Gemma remembered that Greg had told her that he'd fallen over backwards and nearly squashed Baldy. Then she remembered what he said he'd being doing. He'd been hanging Gemma's scarf up!

'AAAAAAAAAAAAAAAAAAHHHHHHHHHHHHH HHHHHAAAAAAAAAAAAAAAAA,' shouted Gemma, even though it was midnight. 'THAT'S IT,' she shouted, again forgetting that it was still the middle of the night. Baldy didn't follow Gemma or Greg - he followed anything that smelled of Seafa. He wasn't following the stupid, penguin, pompom scarf because he liked the pompoms - he was following Seafa's smell. Now a very exciting thought rushed into Gemma's mind. If they could somehow make the competition assault course smell like Seafa, then Baldy would follow the course, and not need food as a treat to get him round it. Gemma lay back down in bed, and thought long and hard about how to make the course super Seafa smelly.

*

BEEP BEEP BEEP BEEP BEEP BEEP, sounded Gemma's alarm. She whacked the top of the clock to make it quiet, wondered what day it was, and snuggled back down into her duvet. Within a second, she remembered that this was no ordinary day. Today was competition day! She shot out of bed. In her pyjamas, she raced to talk to her mum and dad about the new arrangements for today. Yesterday, mum had agreed to take her to the competition to meet Greg, so that she could support him and Baldy. However, she now knew that she needed to see Seafa before going to the competition, so asked her mum if she could take her to Greg's house straight away. Gemma's mum was in the middle of eating breakfast, and didn't appear to want to be rushed at all.

'Please, Mum, it's really important that I get to Greg's early. He doesn't know it, but he's relying on me to help him win the competition,' pleaded Gemma.

'Well, I've just got to finish my bacon and drink my tea and then we can go. Although, you'll look a bit funny turning up at Greg's in your jimjams, sweetie,' joked Gemma's mum. Gemma knew that she should wash, and clean her teeth before getting dressed, but surely one day wouldn't hurt. Anyway, she hadn't eaten anything since she'd cleaned her teeth last night, and really didn't understand why she had to do them again now. She quickly picked up the first clothes that she could find, pulled her hair back into a ponytail and raced back downstairs.

'Ready,' called Gemma running into the kitchen, to find her mum with exactly the same amount of bacon and tea left. She wondered how adults could possibly be so slow! She wanted to pick the bacon up, stuff it into her mouth and eat it herself; she knew she could do it in less than thirty seconds. She also knew that with one gulp she could polish off the tea, too. Why was it taking her mum so long?

'I'm nearly finished, sweetie, I just need to finish

my bacon and my tea and then we can go,' repeated Gemma's mum. *But really, though?* thought Gemma to herself, becoming more and more impatient. Was it *really* so important that her mum should finish her breakfast? Would it make so much difference to the day if she walked away from the table now and got in the car?

'What's that in your hair?' asked Gemma's mum, squinting because she hadn't got her glasses. 'Come here, let me have a closer look.' She beckoned her over, and began to fiddle with the back of her head. She pulled at something that was stuck in Gemma's bobble, and tutted and sighed. 'Why are you wearing an old cough sweet in your hair?' she asked smiling.

'Ha ha ha,' laughed Gemma, remembering that a few days ago, she'd been sucking the sweet, had coughed, and the sweet had shot out of her mouth and she couldn't find it. She knew it would turn up eventually, but really didn't expect it to be in her hair.

'Have you brushed your hair today?' asked her mum, knowing full well that she hadn't.

'I'm in a bit of a rush, I didn't think it would matter for one day,' explained Gemma, hoping that her mum would let her off with it. 'I really need to get to Greg's house. Please can we go now?'

'Face, teeth, hair and then we can go.'

'OK,' replied Gemma who was already halfway up the stairs; she knew there was no use in arguing about it. 'I'll race you. I bet you 10p that you can't finish your bacon, your tea, and find your glasses, before I come back down!' challenged Gemma, hoping that this would encourage her mum to get a move on.

'Bring it on, shorty,' mum replied, she could never resist a challenge. The two of them rushed around like maniacs. Within a minute, mum was standing at the front door with a banana in one hand, and the other hand stretched out in front of her. Gemma saw her as she began running down the stairs; she turned around and ran back into her room to her money box. She quickly shook her money out onto the floor, grabbed 10p, and ran back down the stairs.

'Give me the money now, or I will shoot you with my banana,' demanded Gemma's mum.

'You win,' said Gemma, putting the 10p coin into her mum's hand.

'Breakfast's important, Gemma,' said Mum, handing her the banana.

They left the house to find Gemma's dad in the garage fiddling with his latest invention. He spent many hours dreaming up useful things and making them. Gemma often helped him, and was always willing to test out his new ideas. He regularly made things just for her. One of her favourite things that he'd made was her bedroom curtains. He'd put little tiny LEDs into them and wired them up so that they looked like the curtains that you sometimes find on a stage. She loved these most, because she knew that he'd made them just for her, and no·one else had anything like them in their rooms.

'Morning, come and have a look at what I'm working on today,' called her dad.

'Oh, really sorry, Dad, I'm in a big rush to get to

Greg's house. Please can we do it later?' replied Gemma apologetically.

'Course you can, love, I'll fix it up in the house, and you see if you can spot it when you come home,' said Gemma's dad with a cheeky smile.

'OK,' said Gemma, dashing to get into the car.

*

During the journey, Gemma checked her coat pockets to make sure that she had 0.3.1. It was cold again today, so another perfect day to use it. She messaged Greg to tell him that she was on her way, but already knew that this was a waste of time because he never checked his phone. She ate her banana and put her hair bobble back in. This time it was without the cough sweet, but with a little bit of banana string that had become attached to her hand.

Gemma kissed her mum to say thank you, and ran up the path to Greg's house. *DING DONG, DING DONG, DING DONG.*

'Alright, I'm coming,' called Greg's dad as he ambled to the door, having no idea what all the rush was about.

'Morning,' said Gemma. 'I really need to talk to Greg about the competition please. Is he still here?' she asked, a little out of breath and obviously in a hurry. Greg's dad moved aside and did his usual gesture that told her that she was welcome to come in.

'Thanks,' said Gemma, relieved to know she wasn't too late.

'Gregoryyyyyyyyyyyyyyy, your girlfriend's here,' sniggered Greg's dad. Neither Gemma or Greg found this even slightly amusing, and neither of them could see why adults thought it funny either.

'She's my friend, Dad, *not* my girlfriend,' protested Greg, as he made his way down the stairs.

'I have a plan to help you win the competition,' blurted out Gemma. She really didn't care what Greg's dad called her at the moment; she needed to share her plan, and quick.

'I'm actually feeling quite confident this morning, I'm sure when Baldy sees the trophy, he'll know exactly what to do,' replied Greg.

'Well, I'm sure you're right, but I think that there's something we can do to help Baldy along a bit,' said Gemma, not wanting to ruin Greg's confident mood. She then went on to explain her midnight brainwave, and Greg immediately saw that Baldy had been following Seafa and not Gemma or him.

'Right, I'm going to cuddle next door's cat!' shouted Greg in a very authoritative tone. 'Mum's round there now checking on Santa and Seafa.'

'Good plan,' replied Gemma to Greg's back as he ran down the path.

'Oh, I don't know what all the rush is about, love. Doesn't anyone know it's Saturday and we should be having a rest?' said Greg's dad, sitting at the kitchen table with his tea and newspaper. 'Look, the dog gets more peace and quiet than the humans in this house.' Baldy was sitting in his basket with his head on his paws, staring into space, totally relaxed. Gemma wondered if he had any idea that it was the day of the competition. She wondered if he'd be nervous when he saw the course. Would he fidget and need the loo, like Gemma often did when she was anxious about things?

'Gemma, come quick, Seafa's missing!' shouted Greg from the front door. Without a word, Gemma got up and ran next door.

'Oof, still all rushing around! They'll probably find the blooming cat sitting in front of the fire!' mumbled Greg's dad to Baldy.

'We've looked everywhere for her - she's gone, vanished!' said Greg.

The children spent a couple of minutes talking to Santa. Gemma loved detective work and was very good at asking questions and gathering information. Greg listened, and quietly admired how cool and logical she was. Again, he made another mental note to use her questioning strategy at a later date. It appeared that Seafa had been missing all night. She hadn't eaten the food that had been put out for her yesterday afternoon, and Santa hadn't seen her since Gemma had left. Gemma asked Santa if it was OK if she and Greg looked around the house for her, and he agreed. They decided to split up to make the search quicker, but they kept bumping into each other everywhere, and weren't too systematic about where they'd looked.

'STTTTTOOOOOOOOOOOOOOOOOOP,' shouted Greg. 'I know exactly how we can find Seafa!' He ran out of the front door, shouting, 'I'll be less than a minute, hang on,'

Gemma continued to look anyway. She was starting to worry that perhaps something had happened to her when she'd gone outside for her walk. However, before any more dreadful thoughts could enter her head, she heard Greg talking to someone as he walked up the path. He'd dragged Baldy by his collar from his basket to the end of their path. Then, realising that he could get to Seafa's house, Baldy was now legging it towards Santa's front door like an Olympic sprinter. He rushed into the hallway, stopped and sniffed. He walked into the lounge, stopped and sniffed. He started towards the kitchen, stopped, turned around and bounded up the stairs. The children followed him, but neither of them could keep up. Eventually, they found him in the bathroom, pawing at the washing basket. Gemma got there first, lifted the lid and looked inside. There, curled up on top of a hideous-looking tablecloth, was a cuddly bundle of fluff.

'Oh, look at you!' said Gemma softly. 'We've found her, Greg,' she said trying to whisper and shout all at the same time. 'Well done, Baldy,' Gemma patted the top of his head. All that Baldy could do, was continue to paw at the basket because he was too short to see over the top. Gemma carefully lifted Seafa out of the basket and held her next to Baldy's nose. He rubbed his face against hers and she opened her eyes and meoooowed.

'Fantastic,' shouted Greg. 'Quick, give her to me.' Gemma held Seafa out towards Greg who immediately curled herself around Gemma's neck. Gemma carefully put the fluffy cat back into her arms and tried again. This time she jumped out of Gemma's hands and hid herself behind Baldy.

'Not again!' said Greg, remembering that she wouldn't let him hold her last time he'd tried.

'Right, get that cat and snuggle her,' instructed Greg.

'Ooooooookay,' replied Gemma, a little surprised. Realising that this was not the time to ask questions, she put her hand out to Seafa, who sniffed and slowly walked out from behind Baldy. Gemma gently picked her up and snuggled and kissed her like she always did.

'Brilliant,' shouted Greg. 'Now, rub that cat all over you!'

'What?' asked Gemma, who simply couldn't let this go without asking.

'Pleaaaasseee, just rub her all over you! You'll see why in a minute.'

'Erm, right, OK,' replied Gemma, wondering how she was actually going to 'rub Seafa all over her' as Greg had put it. She played with Seafa and got her to run around her feet and climb up her shirt. Baldy joined in, and Greg watched on in astonishment.

'Baldy has never moved so much in his life!' exclaimed Greg.

'Do you think that's enough? She's climbed all over me,' asked Gemma.

'Perfect, thanks. Now, walk downstairs with Seafa and see if Baldy follows you,' said Greg.

Gemma carried Seafa down the stairs, and of course, Baldy followed her.

'I'll hold onto Baldy's collar while you put Seafa out into the garden. I need to know if Baldy will follow you, when Seafa isn't in your arms, OK?' asked Greg.

'OK, hang onto him then, I'll put her out now. Come on, fluffy, go and have a little play in the garden, you can come back in very soon,' said Gemma stroking Seafa. She carried Seafa out of the back door, closed the door behind her, and popped her down on the grass. Greg held tightly onto Baldy's collar. He tried to explain that Seafa would be back soon, but Baldy wasn't listening.

'Grrrrrrrrrrrrrrrrrrrrrrrrr,' growled Baldy, pulling and tugging Greg towards the back door. 'Grrrrrrrrrrrrrrrrrrrrrrrrrrrrrrrrrrrrrrrrrrrrrrrrrrrr'.

Greg hoped that Gemma would be quick coming back in; he couldn't hold onto Baldy much longer. However, he didn't need to hold Baldy any longer at all, as at that moment, Seafa popped her head through the cat flap, and jumped back into the house. She trotted effortlessly over to Baldy, and snuggled up by his side.

'Ha ha ha ha ha,' laughed Greg; he hadn't expected Seafa to come into the house before Gemma. 'What a very clever cat you are,' he said. Gemma came in just as Greg was laughing and was glad that he could see the funny side.

'I didn't think about the cat flap,' confessed Gemma with a smile. She bent down and locked the cat flap. 'Now, shall we have another go at that?' she asked.

'Yes, but you need to get back in here really quickly. I can't hold onto him for long; he's growling and pulling really hard.'

'OK, I'll only go a little way into the garden and hope I can get back in before she does!' replied Gemma.

Gemma put her hand out to Seafa who jumped into her arms and purred contentedly. Greg held onto Baldy, who began to growl even before Greg had his hand on his collar. Gemma took Seafa outside again, put her down on the grass and ran for the back door. She quickly got inside and closed the door, to be met by Greg and Baldy. Apparently, Baldy had dragged Greg all the way along the hall and into the kitchen.

'He's not a big dog, but he's super strong,' said Greg, explaining that he hadn't been able to stop Baldy from pulling him along Santa's laminate flooring. Greg let go of Baldy, who stopped growling and positioned himself directly beneath the cat flap and sniffed. Seafa was on the other side of the cat flap, and could be heard meooowing gently to come back in.

'OK, walk towards the lounge, let's see if Baldy follows you,' said Greg. Gemma walked down the hall and into the lounge. Baldy didn't move an inch. Greg knew that he could still hear and probably smell Seafa at the cat flap, so why would he follow Gemma? Greg walked into the lounge leaving Baldy pawing at the cat flap. 'Right, this isn't working and we don't have any time left, we'll just have to go with it and hope it works.'

'Go with what?' asked Gemma and Greg's mum together.

'Gemma, go upstairs and take your clothes off,' demanded Greg.

'I beg YOUR PARDON,' said Greg's mum, whose voice was getting louder and louder and higher and higher with each word.

Gemma stood still, looking at everyone, feeling confused and a little worried.

'GREGORY,' screeched his mum, even louder and higher.

'Erm, erm, oh dear, erm,' replied Greg, very flustered. 'Erm, let me explain.'

'I THINK YOU BETTER HAD, YOUNG MAN!' said his mum. Now, her eyebrows looked like they were trying to escape off the top of her head.

Greg quickly explained that Gemma's clothes smelled like Seafa because she'd been cuddling her. He went on to explain that Baldy followed Gemma whenever Seafa had snuggled with her, and that if he wore Gemma's clothes, Baldy might follow him.

'Why don't you cuddle Seafa yourself?' asked Greg's mum.

'Becauuuuusssse,' said Greg, who was becoming more and more concerned about being late for the competition. 'Becaaaaauuuuuuse, she won't come to me, she won't let me hold her at all.'

'It's true, she doesn't let me hold her either. Gemma has a special touch, just like Mrs Santa,' chipped in Santa.

'So, you see, if I wear Gemma's clothes, Baldy might follow me, and then we might win the trophy and and, and...' Greg's voice trailed off.

'Oh I see, I forgot it was the competition today,' said Greg's mum casually.

'MUM, please can we get a move on? We need to be there in an hour, please can we get moving? I really don't want to be late. Baldy needs to be as relaxed as possible!' said Greg, in a very stressed voice.

'OK, love, I'm coming now. I've put Seafa's food and water out, Santa, I'll pop in again later. What time does the competition finish?' asked his mum.

'I don't know, but I know it starts in an hour!' said Greg, getting more and more agitated about the time.

'Would you like to join us for dinner tonight, Santa?' asked Greg's mum. 'We'll need to be flexible about the time, but I'm guessing that the competition won't go on after five o'clock. We're having shepherd's pie!' Both Gemma and Greg wondered why anyone would accept an invitation to eat shepherd's pie. Pizza or fish and chips or nuggets maybe, but shepherd's pie?

'Oh, yes please, that'll be lovely. I need something to take my mind off...' Santa's voice trailed off and so did his smile.

'Right you are then, I'll let you know when we're home.'

'MUM, please can we get going now?' pleaded Greg. 'Will you help me to get Baldy into the car? He's pining for Seafa at the back door and I don't like it when he growls at me.'

'You just have to show him who's boss,' replied his mum, getting out of her seat and walking to the back door. 'Come on, Baldy, it's time for you to show off! It's the big day, lad.' Greg's mum bent down and held

Baldy's collar. She continued to talk to him and pulled a little to let him know that, apparently, she was boss. Baldy reluctantly stood up, gave a half-hearted growl, and plodded as slowly as he could at her side.

'Put him straight in the car, please. It'll take too long to get him in the house, and then into the car,' requested Greg.

'OK, run ahead and open the car door then. Gemma, you let Seafa back into the house when Baldy's in the car.'

'Oh yes, OK,' replied Gemma, having forgotten that Seafa was locked outside.

*

With Baldy in the car and everyone else now back at Greg's house, it was time for Greg to bring up the awkward clothes swap again.

'Gemma, please can we swap clothes? I know it's odd but you can see how it could work can't you?' pleaded Greg.

'Yes, it's not exactly what I had in mind this morning, but I think it's our only chance now,' replied Gemma.

'Right then, I'd better find Gemma something to wear,' said Greg's mum. 'It'll have to be something belonging to Greg because all of my stuff will be miles too big. Go into the bathroom and I'll hand you some stuff to try on, OK, love?'

'OK,' replied Gemma, wondering what on earth she would soon be wearing.

*

Within a few minutes, everyone, except for Greg's mum was changed, already wearing their coats, standing in the hall waiting to get into the car.

'Has anyone seen the car keys?' shouted Greg's mum, doing her usual picking stuff up and putting stuff down, to find what she'd lost.

'MUM, how can you have lost them? You only had them five minutes ago when you put Baldy into the car!' exclaimed Greg.

'Ah,' said his mum, reaching into her jeans pocket and pulling out the keys. 'Found them,' she said, rushing into the hall, not really wanting to say that she'd had them in her pocket all along. 'Ready then?'

'YES,' stressed Greg, 'let's get going!'

Everyone piled out of the house and into the car.

'Right, we're all set, wagons roll,' announced Greg's mum as usual.

'Yes, please, make this wagon roll,' pleaded Greg.

Baldy sat in the back of the car between the children. Greg watched him throughout the entire journey to see if he was sniffing, or wanting to sit closer to him than to Gemma. But he didn't seem to be bothered about where he sat. He stared out of the front window without a care in the world, while Greg's tummy rolled over and over, as his nerves kicked in.

'What will I do if he won't follow me around the course?' asked Greg.

'Just do your best; I'm sure some of the other dogs

will have minds of their own too,' replied Gemma, trying to help.

'What if he just stands there and ignores me?' asked Greg, who was becoming more and more uncomfortable with his nerves.

'Let's concentrate on the positives. Baldy has perfect balance, he happily goes through the tunnel, and manages all of the jumps without ever knocking off a single pole. He'll do it perfectly today, I'm sure he will,' said Gemma, actually having no idea at all if Baldy would shift himself out of the car, let alone around the course.

Chapter 19

Time to Back Out?

As they arrived at the arena, it was clear that this competition was a big deal. The car park was packed, and this didn't help Greg's nerves at all.

'Oh my goodness, how many people are there here?' asked Greg, astonished by the amount of people milling around.

'Lots - I didn't know there was this much interest in performing dogs,' replied his mum.

'Right, Baldy, let's get this straight,' said Greg, using his most determined voice. 'We've come here to take that lovely, shiny trophy home, right, lad? We've done all the practising we could do, you can make all of the jumps, and we can win, got it?' Baldy shuffled around a little, wagged his tail, and got ready to settle his head down for a snooze. 'C'mon, lad, let's do this!' exclaimed Greg, attaching Baldy's lead and opening the car door. Greg tugged on the lead to tell him to get out of the car. Baldy slowly lumbered out, and plodded along with the rest of the family towards the registration desk.

'Name of exhibitor?' said a greying old man, with about as much personality as a piece of dried-up carrot.

'Erm, erm, is that me or the dog?' asked Greg, not understanding the question at all.

'That is you! Seeing as a dog is not allowed in the arena, and knows nothing about antique furniture!' replied the snooty old man, who was now looking down his long nose and raising his eyebrows.

'I don't know anything about antique furniture either,' replied Greg, feeling thoroughly confused.

'Then, what are you here for?' asked the man, whose nose appeared to be getting longer and longer with each sentence.

'We're here for the competition, Baldy's going to win the trophy!' said Greg, pointing down to Baldy, who couldn't be seen from behind the man's table.

'In that case, you're in the wrong place, young man. You need to be around the other side of the building. There are two arenas here. There is an antiques fair in this arena today; the dog thing must be in the other arena on the east side. Do you know how to get there?' replied the man, now showing his crooked teeth through a very thin smile.

'Erm, no, is it far?' asked Greg, becoming worried about the time again.

'It will take you approximately three minutes if you follow my instructions exactly,' said the man, who then went on to reel off about seventeen different instructions that no one could keep up with.

'OK, thank you,' said Greg, not really sure if he was grateful or not as he left the table and shouted for his mum and dad to follow him. Luckily, as they walked they saw other people with dogs on leads, so decided to follow them, assuming that they knew the way. They arrived at another registration point within a couple of minutes.

'Morning, what's the name of your lovely little Jack Russell?' asked the altogether different man at this registration desk.

'It's Baldy, well, actually it's Jack, but we all call him Baldy,' replied Greg nervously.

'So, would you like him to be introduced as Baldy or Jack?' asked the smiley man with much straighter teeth and a much shorter nose than the antiques man.

'Oh, Baldy, please. He doesn't really know he's called Jack,' replied Greg, all the time thinking to himself that he rarely answers to Baldy either. The man asked a few more questions and told Greg that Baldy was number seventeen and to listen out for their name to be called.

'Good. Baldy's registered, you can go and get him ready now, good luck,' chirped the man, who stood up to peer at Baldy over the registration desk. 'Oh, he's a lovely, little thing, isn't he?'

Baldy and his crew of mum, dad, Gemma and Greg, made their way to the arena and got their first glimpse of the actual course. Gemma was carefully comparing everything on the real course to the one that Greg had made in his garden. She concluded that Baldy should be fine with the obstacles, if he moved at all! However, all that Greg could see was the bright, shiny, silver trophy that stood proudly on the medals table at the back of the arena.

'Look at it, Gem, isn't it fantastic?' said Greg.

'Well, he can certainly do it, there isn't a jump there

that he can't make,' replied Gemma.

'Oh, I haven't looked at the course yet,' said Greg, coming to his senses. 'I was talking about the trophy!'

Gemma chuckled. *As long as he still has his eye on the prize,* she thought to herself.

Greg found where they needed to sit and watched what everyone else was doing. It was fair to say that, as this was Baldy's first competition, none of the family had a clue what to do, so they looked around for ideas from the other dog owners. It appeared that they should have brought a small table to stand Baldy on, while they brushed him and fiddled about with each individual hair on his body. All of the dogs looked like they'd been to the hairdresser's and none of them smelled. Baldy was lying on the floor underneath Gemma's seat. Greg looked down at him and compared him to the other dogs. He looked his usual self, which, to be honest, was a normal dog. He hadn't had a bath in a few weeks, and he was currently lying in a patch of hot chocolate that someone had spilt on the floor. He looked happy enough, but he wasn't sparkling like the other dogs. Greg wondered if he should back out now. Baldy wasn't wearing a diamond-encrusted collar and he didn't smell like a perfume factory; he was just an ordinary dog sitting underneath a chair.

'I think I've made a mistake,' said Greg sadly.

'Why, what's wrong?' asked Gemma concerned.

'Look at them all, being brushed and sprayed and clipped and polished,' said Greg, pointing at the dog-grooming area. Directly opposite them was a small white dog having it's claws manicured. The lady doing it was wearing a proper uniform and was actually polishing the dog's claws. Greg couldn't believe it; didn't that dog ever dig holes in the garden or chase next door's cat?

'I didn't know that Baldy had to be pampered to death. I thought he just had to be able to do the course, and I'm not even sure that he'll do that!' exclaimed Greg, who was beginning to panic.

'Don't worry, let's just watch what happens and hope that Baldy copies the other dogs. Baldy is Baldy, and we love him as he is. He doesn't need to be sprayed or clipped, he's lovely,' replied Gemma.

'Yes, yes, you're right. I'm going to be proud of him no matter what,' said Greg, regaining his determination and faith in Baldy. Greg's mum went to fetch some hot drinks and snacks for lunch - it was still freezing outside and she said that the hot drinks would help to keep them warm while they watched the competition. Gemma remembered that she'd got 0.3.1 in her pocket and quickly popped it on before the dreaded bulbous red-nosed-ness set in.

'Attention, all participants, there are two minutes remaining for competition preparations, two minutes to take your seats, thank you', came a voice over the PA system. All of the dog groomers began to clear away their brushes and sprays, and people started to settle into their seats. Most of the dogs had blankets, laps or cushions to sit on, unlike Baldy, who had created his own comfortable, but messy, hot chocolate bed.

'Category One – champion dog league. Dog number one, Shep, please,' came the voice over the loudspeaker again. The room fell completely silent, and a lady with a fluffy brown and white dog walked into the centre of the arena and bowed to the crowd. Shep stood with his head held very high, and looked like he was standing on tiptoes. Everyone clapped until they heard a high-pitched *BEEEEEEP.* Again, the room fell silent, and Shep and his owner walked to the first obstacle on the course. Shep stood obediently still by his owner's side, until she shouted 'HUP,' when he sprang into action following her perfectly. The owner ran quickly around the course, giving directions with her hands and her voice. Shep, jumped and twisted and balanced and perched wonderfully, without putting a foot or hair out of line. Greg watched, open-mouthed and bewildered by the speed and ease with which Shep completed the course. He knew that even with some kind of miracle, poor Baldy could not compete with Shep.

'Come on,' he said to Gemma and his mum and dad. 'Baldy doesn't stand a chance against Shep, or any of these other dogs - we might as well go home now.'

'Noooo,' said his mum, 'I'm enjoying watching this. I never imagined it would be so good!'

'We can always stay and just watch. It'll give you an idea of what's expected, in case you decide to enter Baldy next year, maybe when he's a bit more ready,' said Gemma, trying to cheer up a very, very miserable Greg. Greg made no reply and continued to watch, as dog after dog completed the course faultlessly. Shep was by no means the best dog there; they were all spectacular and perfectly groomed. Greg wondered how the judges could possibly decide on who the winner would be.

'Category Two – mature dog league. Dog number twelve, Charlie, please,' came the next announcement. Charlie was a dark brown, short-haired sausage dog. He yapped as he took to the arena, then his owner bent down, whispered something in his ear, and he stood completely still to take his bow. Again, Charlie, like all the other dogs, completed the course without a single mistake. He was a little slower than some of the other dogs but he jumped and balanced with style and grace. The rest of the dogs in category two were all brilliant, and Greg continued to watch and worry as it got closer and closer to Baldy's turn.

'Category Three – newcomer league. Dog number seventeen, Baldy, please,' came the next announcement. Without a word, Greg stood up, took off his coat and walked Baldy, who was still on his lead, into the centre of the arena. Baldy sniffed at the floor as he walked and when he arrived in the centre, sat down with his head on his paws as if to take yet another nap. Greg bowed amongst giggles and applause, and even Gemma laughed out loud when she saw him. Greg's bright red trousers, or more correctly Gemma's trousers, were at least ten centimetres too short for him and looked completely ridiculous. He'd put his football shorts over the top of the trousers, because he hadn't been able to do the button or the zip up, and in such a rush couldn't come up with a better solution. Gemma's T-shirt was also at least four sizes too small for him as well, and it was bright pink with 'girlpower' written across the front. Luckily Greg hadn't had time to notice the heart of pink sequins on the back. To finish off his look, Greg had Gemma's stupid, penguin, pompom scarf tied around his wrist; he couldn't fit it around his neck, so thought this was the next best thing to do with it.

'Ohhhhh, my goodness, ohhhhhhhhh nooooooooooo, what does our Greg look like, ohhhhhhhh my goodness,' said Greg's mum in utter shock and disbelief at what she saw.

BEEEEEEP. The room fell silent and it was Baldy's big moment. Gemma sat on the edge of her chair, hoping and praying that Baldy would follow Greg to the first obstacle. Greg, head held high like a championship dog, began to walk to the start of the course.

'Please take the competitors lead off - the course has to be completed without a lead, thank you,' came the voice over the loudspeaker. Undeterred, Greg slowly bent down and took off Baldy's lead. In complete silence, he then continued to walk toward the start of the course. Baldy stayed exactly where he was, and Gemma's heart began to pound.

'Come on, Baldy, come on, move, Baldy,' willed Gemma under her breath. 'Mooooooooooovee, dog, moooooove.'

Nothing, absolutely nothing; Baldy remained where he was, unaware that everyone in the arena was waiting for him. Greg began to look nervous and looked to his mum, hoping that she would give him some idea of what to do next. However, she was still utterly shocked by how her son was dressed, and was sitting, with her hand across her mouth, trying to stop her shock from coming out. Gemma, noticing Greg's discomfort, moved her arm to tell Greg to dangle the scarf, so that Baldy might pick up on Seafa's scent. Greg had no idea what she was doing so he just stood there. He stood, wearing too-small girls' clothes, in the middle of an arena full of people with his head high, doing nothing. He could hear his heartbeat getting faster and faster and louder and louder in his head as he waited. The palms of his hands began to sweat and he got hotter and hotter. People in the arena began to whisper quietly amongst themselves, as Greg's face became red and flustered.

'Baldy,' shouted Greg, realising that he had to do something now. Baldy raised his eyebrows and lifted his head. Greg, called him again, while lifting his pompom-scarf arm and motioning Baldy to come and stand at his side. Baldy, very slowly shuffled his feet and placed his nose back onto his paws and closed his eyes. Gemma was squirming in her seat, as she watched her friend go through the whole embarrassing ordeal.

As moments passed, Greg's head became lower and lower until he was looking at the floor, no longer able to hold it high. The crowd began to slowly applaud, and Greg took Baldy's lead out of his pocket, knowing that this time he was defeated. He regained his composure, took a deep breath and mentally prepared himself for dragging Baldy out of the centre of the arena. However, as he began to raise his eyes from the floor, he noticed something out of the corner of his eye. Baldy was standing at his heel! He was exactly where he should be. While Greg had been sweating and embarrassed, Baldy had trotted over and stood by his side. The audience had started to applaud when Baldy was obedient, but Greg thought that they were applauding slowly to ask him to leave. Baldy looked up at Greg with his lovely, doggy eyes and wagged his tail.

'Good boy, Baldy, good dog,' said Greg, a little unsure of what to do next. So he decided to copy all of the other dog owners! 'Hup,' shouted Greg, holding out his arm to show Baldy where to go. Baldy looked at Greg like he'd gone mad, and didn't budge. Greg began to run by the side of the first obstacle which was a low balancing beam, like the benches he used in PE. Baldy obediently ran in Greg's footsteps, following him on the floor, along the side of the obstacle. The audience began to laugh and applaud, and Greg couldn't help but smile that Baldy had actually followed him, even if it was along the floor, instead of across the obstacle. Baldy loved the applause; he wagged his tail and put his front paws onto Greg's knee.

Greg patted him and decided to take him back to the beginning of the course to try again. He knew he wasn't going to win the trophy, so he might as well give Baldy another chance at the obstacles. Greg ran back to the beginning and still, miraculously, Baldy followed him. He bent down and gently told Baldy that he should have another go. Baldy looked up at him with his dark eyes and wagged his tail. Greg then began to run along side the obstacle just as he had done before, and Baldy also did exactly what he had done before; he bypassed the balancing beam and ran directly in Greg's footsteps. By now, the audience were really starting to enjoy themselves. All of the previous contestants had been serious trophy chasers. They were all very professional and polished and, well, frankly, boring. Baldy and Greg offered a new angle to the competition. They were funny, entertaining and natural. The atmosphere in the arena had completely changed, the pressure felt by all the previous competitors to be one hundred percent perfect had vanished, and the whole room relaxed and enjoyed. Even Gemma sat back and joined in with the laughter.

So, having had huge success with Baldy following him, Greg decided to go all out. He wasn't at all sure about what he was going to do next, but there were many things he'd not been sure about today - why stop now? He ran back to the beginning of the course again, with Baldy following him beautifully. He got down on his hands and knees, and patted and stroked Baldy, whilst telling him exactly what he was going to do. His final words to Baldy before starting the course again were, 'Please, lad, do this for me or I'm gonna look a right idiot.' Greg then stood still with Baldy at his heel, shouted 'Hup' and began the course again. However, this time, Greg pretended to be the dog! He carefully walked along the balance beam and Baldy followed him. He jumped through the low hoop and Baldy followed him. The crowd were in stitches; they were clapping and cheering - everyone was captivated by Greg's alternative methods. There he was, wearing girls' clothing that was far too small, running over obstacles made for dogs, being applauded and cheered.

The funniest part of the course was, without doubt, the tunnel. It was a fabric construction and looked a bit like a large spring covered in material. Greg got down onto his tummy and began crawling through the tunnel, commando-style. Baldy followed him inside, and instantly started growling. It was a lot darker and longer than the tunnel that Greg had made in the garden, and apparently Baldy wasn't keen! First Greg's head popped out of the end, shortly followed by his shoulders, and then Baldy's nose appeared. Baldy had been so frightened in the tunnel that he'd climbed onto Greg's back and Greg had had to crawl through for both of them. As soon as Baldy saw that they were almost out of the tunnel and back into the daylight, he sprang off Greg's back, over his head and out of the tunnel, leaving Greg still having to crawl to get his legs out. Again, the crowd cheered and clapped; they'd never seen anything quite like this before.

Greg continued to use the same strategy to get Baldy around the rest of the course, and the audience continued to appreciate watching them. However, he came across a slight glitch when he reached the final obstacle. This was the one where the dogs got to show off their jumping ability. In front of Greg, was a hoop, hanging off what could only be described as a free-standing door frame. It was hanging just higher than his head, and he knew that there was absolutely no way that he could jump through it. So, having no other ideas in mind, he resorted to running alongside the hoop to see if Baldy might just make the connection for himself. Of course, he didn't! He continued to follow Greg around the outside of the hoop. At that point, Greg was so pleased with what Baldy had achieved, it no longer mattered if he jumped through the hoop or not. He'd completed most of the course and Greg was overjoyed. Especially when he thought about how he had felt, standing in the arena with his head to the floor wondering how he was ever going to live down the embarrassment of dragging Baldy out by his lead. So, with that thought, he ran over to where the judges were seated, took his bow just like the polished and perfect contestants had done, and began to leave the arena with Baldy walking obediently at his side. The audience were still clapping, and many were standing and cheering.

Greg looked over to where Gemma and his mum and dad were sitting, and saw them standing, smiling and clapping him and Baldy. Greg's dad punched the air in celebration, and Greg copied him, thrusting his arm into the air like a footballer who had just scored the winning goal. But, as he did this, the stupid, penguin, pompom scarf that was tied around his wrist, went flying through the air. It flew across the arena, passed the balance beam, passed the tunnel and through the final hoop. Before Greg had properly noticed where it had landed, Baldy had run across the arena, passed the balance beam, passed the tunnel and swiftly jumped through the hoop to collect the scarf.

The audience exploded with applause at this surprise finale. Baldy, who was shocked by the sudden noise, jumped back through the hoop and straight back to Greg's heel. So, not only had Baldy showed that he could jump through the hoop, he'd done it twice and returned directly to Greg with his scarf. Greg got down and rubbed Baldy's ears to congratulate him on his spectacular performance. They casually walked side by side out of the arena, to be met with hand shakes and pats from the front row members of the audience. They reached their seats to find Gemma and his dad smiling from ear to ear, his mum still had her hands over her mouth; she was crying with pride. Gemma, Greg and his dad performed a family high five, while his mum ferreted about in the bottom of her handbag to find a tissue that wasn't already covered in snot. As it turned out, she couldn't find one, so her face continued to be covered in snot and mascara until Greg's dad noticed and gave her his tissue. Baldy, casually slid himself underneath Gemma's seat, and made himself comfortable in his hot chocolate bed. Greg, put his coat on, and looked at the trophy. He knew that he and Baldy wouldn't be taking it home, but he couldn't have felt any more proud than he did now. With or without a trophy, Baldy had completed the course and Greg was over the moon.

The rest of the dogs that competed after Baldy were also newcomers. One of them stood in the centre of the arena, yapping and chasing his own tail and his owner couldn't make him stop at all. He ended up being carried back to his seat. Another dog, freaked out in the tunnel. He was so scared that he sat down in the middle and was unable to move. After trying several times, and failing to coax him out, his owner eventually tipped the tunnel up and slid him out like he was on some kind of fairground ride. The poor pooch left the arena with his hair standing on end, and his little legs shaking helplessly.

The final dog to compete was an over-sized German shepherd dog. His jumping skills were fantastic; he could jump very high, making it look almost effortless. However, he really struggled with the balance parts of the course and constantly fell off the beam and the see-saw like he was drunk. Every time he fell off, he got back up and did exactly the same thing again, making no improvement at all.

Gemma and Greg both knew that they shouldn't

giggle, but by the end of the German shepherd dog's round, they were both crying hysterically with laughter. Greg's mum was poking them to tell them to stop laughing, but she found this very difficult, as she couldn't really stop herself from laughing either. Again, the snot-covered tissue made an appearance, but this time she tried to share it with Greg. To protect himself, he instantly covered his face with the stupid, pompom, penguin scarf and noticed that it did in fact smell of something. He wasn't sure if what he smelt was Seafa, but it did smell of something. He decided to smell the rest of himself to see if Gemma's t-shirt and trousers smelt the same, so he put his head inside his coat and sniffed.

Gemma nudged Greg's mum, who nudged his dad and they all looked on, while Greg did his incredible headless man impersonation. Not having recovered from the drunken dog episode, it had all become too much for Greg's mum. She'd experienced so many emotions during the last half an hour that finally, she had cracked. She let out an enormous laugh, which attracted the attention of many other people sitting close by. Greg also wondered what was going on and popped his head out of his coat to investigate. Little did he know that Gemma, his mum, his dad and half of the audience, were looking at him again because of his odd actions.

'What?' said Greg, not realising how funny a headless person looked. 'What's so funny?' Gemma and Greg's dad both popped their heads inside their coats, exactly like Greg had done, to show him what he looked like. Greg had to admit it did look pretty funny. But what was even funnier, was when the other people in the audience around them, joined in too. There were about fifteen adults and children with their heads popped inside their coats. Greg had once again inspired a party atmosphere, and everyone was laughing and having fun. Until, that is, they heard this:-

'Attention please, ladies, gentlemen, children and canine stars. After much consideration and debate, the judges have unanimously decided on a winner for this year's trophy.'

The room fell silent, and the tension that everyone felt when the competition had first started returned and filled the room. Every person had their eyes fixed on the shiny trophy that was now standing on a table in the centre of the arena.

'This year it has been a very close competition. The standard has risen again, and it has been extremely difficult to judge,' said a woman who herself had hair like a toy poodle dog. 'Without further ado, let us announce our winner, and present this fantastic trophy. The winner of this year's competition is... POPPY, owned and trained by Olivia Sharma!'

The room exploded once again, as Poppy and Olivia went into the arena to receive their prize. The beautiful, silver trophy was presented to Olivia, who beamed with pride, holding her prize, which was almost as big as herself. Over recent weeks Greg had imagined over and over again, that it would be Baldy's name being read out at this point. He'd imagined himself holding the trophy and posing for the cameras. However, he was not in the least disappointed that Poppy had won; he knew that Baldy wasn't up to that standard and didn't regret entering the competition at all. In fact, if anything, he was inspired. He'd always thought that Baldy was a clever dog, and today, watching the other dogs do so well, had inspired him to carry on training him, to see how good he could become. Greg was pleased that maybe someday, Baldy and he might walk into the centre of the arena to claim the trophy. While he was daydreaming about what might have been, people had started to chat and pack up their things. There was another announcement, that could only just be heard over the shuffling of chairs and feet.

'Our runner-up prizes have been equally difficult to judge. The standard was exceptionally high in all categories. However, the judges have made their decision and...the Category Two winner is Bruno and Category Three winner is Jack. Could dogs and owners please come to the centre of the arena for their presentation.' The audience settled down a little, as a ripple of applause began for the other category winners. Then, a further announcement was made. 'Oh, I beg your pardon, just to clarify, our Category Three winner is Jack, who performed today as, and answers very obediently to the name of Baldy.' Once again, Greg's mum's hand was across her mouth. His dad nudged Gemma, who in turn nudged Greg.

'Greg, you and Baldy, you've wooooooooooonnnnnnnnnn

nnn!' shouted Gemma.

Greg was too astonished to speak. He looked under Gemma's chair at Baldy, and stood up.

'Come on, Baldy, you're a winner, lad, I knew you could do it, come on.'

Baldy stared at Greg with his usual blank expression. 'Come on, lad,' said Greg, hoping that Baldy would rise to the occasion just once more. Greg began to walk away but Baldy continued to sit.

'Use the scarf,' said Gemma, realising that Baldy had no motivation to move. Greg pulled the stupid, pompom, penguin scarf from his pocket, dangled it by Baldy's nose, and began to walk again. This time, Baldy followed him, and Greg marched them both proudly into the middle of the arena. The officials and judges shook hands with Greg and Baldy, and then the prizes were awarded. To Greg's complete delight he was given a very small, shiny, silver trophy; it was about the size of his hand. He also received a certificate that had a piece of red ribbon wrapped around it. Even though it wasn't the trophy that Greg had set out to win, he was extremely proud of it. The photographers came and asked Greg to smile and hold up the trophy. They asked if they could have a family photo, so he called his mum, dad and Gemma into the arena to have their photos taken too. His mum was still overcome, but fiddled about with her hair to try to make herself presentable for the photo. Greg's dad was obviously very proud; he stuck his chest out and smiled broadly. Gemma remembered to quickly remove 0.3.1 just before the photo was taken, and Greg held the trophy up and smiled. Baldy sat beautifully in the middle of them all, not really having much of a clue about what was going on. The photographer was from the local newspaper. He told Greg that the competition was going to be featured in the sports section of tonight's edition, and that he had to dash to email his photos and report.

'Can't make any promises, mate, but I'll see if we can get your name and picture in tonight,' said the photographer, as he rushed away to his car.

'Wow, Baldy, we're going to be in the newspaper!' exclaimed Greg. 'I'm so proud of you.'

Chapter 20

Shepherd's Pie

Everyone talked non-stop in the car all the way home, except for Baldy, who, for one, can't speak, and two, wouldn't have spoken anyway because he was fast asleep. They chatted about everything that had happened, the moments of despair and moments of relief. Gemma told Greg that she had wanted to run into the arena to rescue him when Baldy wouldn't move. Greg said that at that moment he was wishing that a large hole would have appeared at his feet, so that he could have jumped into it to avoid further embarrassment. As they arrived home, Greg asked his mum if Gemma could stay for a while longer. He really wanted to get the newspaper to read the report, and to see if the pictures had made it in there.

'Course she can, love, she's always welcome,' replied Greg's mum, who had finally managed to compose herself, and hadn't cried at all in the last ten minutes.

*

Once inside, Greg's mum busied herself making dinner, while the children looked online to see if anyone had posted anything about the competition yet. Olivia and Poppy had posted a small blog about their epic win, but there was no mention of Baldy or any other dogs. Santa came round and asked if it was alright if Seafa joined them for dinner too. Baldy shot out of his basket to Seafa's side; they sniffed each other and rubbed noses. Baldy trotted off to his basket and Seafa followed him. He lay down comfortably and Seafa got into the basket too. She walked around in a circle a couple of times, found a comfy spot and snuggled in next to Baldy.

'Ahhhhhh,' said Greg. 'Ahh, Gem, look at them,' he said, showing his emotional side.

'Listen to you!' exclaimed Gemma, giggling. 'Yesterday you were trying to get rid of her, today she's all "ahhhhhhh"' said Gemma, mimicking Greg.

'Yeah well, Seafa should get a certificate and a trophy really, because Baldy and I couldn't have done it without her,' replied Greg, smiling at Baldy and Seafa in their little love nest.

'Dinner's ready,' called his mum from the kitchen. Greg and Gemma rushed to set the dining room table. Greg's mum had asked them to do it about half an hour ago, but they'd been busy looking for the competition winners online and had forgotten.

*

Everyone gathered around the dinner table, except for Greg's dad who was now apparently missing.

'Go and see if you can find your dad, he can't be far away,' said Greg's mum. Greg wandered into the lounge, then up the stairs calling his dad as he went. There was no sign of him at all. Until, that is, when he came bursting into the house waving the newspaper in the air.

'It's in! Greg, it's in the paper!' shouted his dad, who showed more excitement now, than Greg had ever seen before. He spread the newspaper out onto the dining table so that everyone could see. There was a photo of Poppy and Olivia in the middle of the back page. Poppy was sitting inside the enormous trophy with her head popping out of the top; it was a very cute picture. There was a photo and a brief write-up to the left of Poppy's picture, all about the winner of the mature dog category. And then, on the right hand side at the bottom of the page was team Baldy.

For a moment, there was complete silence as everyone looked closely at the picture. One by one, first Greg's mum, then Greg, then his dad, all started to chuckle. Greg was in the centre of the photo wearing a ridiculously small girl's outfit and a huge grin. Dad had his chest puffed out like a championship wrestler, and his mum's nose was Rudolph-red. Gemma was wearing a pair of jeans that had been rolled up around the waist and the bottoms, to stop her from treading on them, coupled with a dark blue hoody with the slogan 'Badboy,' written across the front. Baldy was sitting in the middle of them all, perfectly poised, but with his eyes closed; he must have blinked as the flash went off.

'What a bunch of misfits,' said Greg's mum, glaring at the photo. 'Look at the state of my nose - I'll be getting a visit from Father Christmas soon asking for help with his deliveries!'

'Are you busy on the evening of the twenty-fourth of December? I have a very special job for you,' joked Santa.

'I need one of those thingies I think, Gemma, the nose thingies that you've got. I can't walk around looking like that,' said Greg's mum, shocked by her own photo.

'I can make one for you if you'd like - it's my own design,' said Gemma proudly.

'Yes please, love, looking at that photo, I need all the help I can get!' replied Greg's mum, shaking her head and walking away to fetch dinner.

Over dinner they read through the review of the competition, which was fairly accurate. The reporter had commented that Greg and Baldy had brought their own imaginative style to this year's competition, and judging by the photo, there was no denying that.

'Mum, do you make shepherd's pie out of German shepherd dogs?' asked Greg, grinning, while shovelling in another forkful. This immediately made them think of the drunken dog that fell sideways off all the obstacles, and everyone was in hysterics again. Gemma wasn't quite ready for

Greg's funny comment. She had just taken a mouthful of her drink and was now in great danger of spitting it all over the place as she couldn't contain her laughter. She spluttered, and a little trickle of juice ran down her chin.

Greg looked at her and knew what was about to happen, and this made him laugh even more. However, he was in a worse position than Gemma, with his mouthful of shepherd's pie about to escape at high speed, at any moment. Gemma tried to look away, but heard Greg gurgling and couldn't help but look at him. Trying very hard to keep his lips sealed, Greg gulped in an attempt to swallow his pie. He made a loud drain-like noise, and this proved too much for both of them. Juice and shepherd's pie came flying out of their mouths, followed immediately by very sorry sorries, as they looked to Greg's mum. Greg knew that she would be cross, especially as they had Santa with them as a guest for dinner.

However, to their utter surprise, Greg's mum was completely helpless herself; her shoulders were shaking with laughter and, once again, she had her hand over her mouth, suffering with the same problem that the children had just experienced. She managed to contain herself; swallowed her food and apologised to everyone, and especially to Santa for their disgraceful table manners.

'You know,' said Santa, 'I'm so happy to be amongst laughter, I don't have a clue what you're all laughing about, but it feels wonderful, and I wouldn't have missed this for the world. You've cheered me up no end, thank you.' Again, everyone started to titter, partly because they were all already gripped by the giggles, but also because Santa had a small clump of shepherd's pie wagging in his beard as he talked.

Even though the children would never have usually chosen shepherd's pie for dinner, tonight it proved to be a treat that was thoroughly enjoyed by all.

'Do you think you'll enter the competition again next year?' asked Gemma.

'What do you think?' replied Greg, as he smiled at a snoozing Baldy and Seafa.

Acknowledgments

La, you know what you said, I'm so grateful x

Potter, thanks for taking this journey with me, your help and support have been invaluable x

Thank you to Alex, Kian and Reece. Yes, I did write the story... now you can find out the ending!

Thanks to editor Becca, cover artist Francesca, and internal images artist Clare. Thank you to my beta readers. Thank you, Kath, for your expert help and advice on formatting and publishing.

It was a pleasure working with you all. Let's do it again!

About the Author

Lottie has had a variety of jobs and interests. She started off as an accounts assistant, but that didn't suit her as it was too much of a sit-down job. She really had fun as a painter and decorator. Being up a ladder is much more her style! She took great pleasure in looking after her own children while they were growing up, and also other people's children, when she worked as a primary school teacher.

For the time being, she can be found enjoying her days in her tiny coffee shop, chatting to friendly people, and dreaming up new plots and characters for further stories. Lottie measures her success by her happiness. Right now, she's feeling content, therefore successful.

Printed in Great Britain
by Amazon